He needed a new kind of woman!

That was the answer. Mike would be more selective. Discriminating. He would set certain standards and abide by them. No more blundering into relationships based on chemistry. No more being seduced by a woman's needing him. No more getting attached to children that were no concern of his.

Digging through his catch-all drawer, Mike pulled out a notepad and wrote:

Mike Calder's Minimum Requirements for a Woman

1. She will have a good job.
2. No children.
3. Doesn't believe men are a scourge upon the earth.
4. Drives a new car.
5. Lives in an apartment or condo.

Pleased with his efforts, Mike skimmed the list again. Just one last thing—

6. Sexy.

Glenda Sanders has always wanted to do on-the-job research, and she's finally had her chance with *Not This Guy!* "However," she says, laughing, "it wasn't anything as exciting as going to a tropical island or being jilted—I just made frequent trips to the veterinarian." Glenda lives in Florida with her husband, son and her pets— her dog, Penny, and her cat, TW Dumpster— who didn't appreciate having to see their neighborhood vet quite so often!

Books by Glenda Sanders

HARLEQUIN TEMPTATION

Don't miss any of our special offers. Write to us at the following address for information on our newest releases.

Harlequin Reader Service
U.S.: 3010 Walden Ave., P.O. Box 1325, Buffalo, NY 14269
Canadian: P.O. Box 609, Fort Erie, Ont. L2A 5X3

Glenda Sanders
NOT THIS GUY!

Harlequin Books

TORONTO • NEW YORK • LONDON
AMSTERDAM • PARIS • SYDNEY • HAMBURG
STOCKHOLM • ATHENS • TOKYO • MILAN
MADRID • WARSAW • BUDAPEST • AUCKLAND

ISBN 0-373-25647-7

NOT THIS GUY!

1

MIKE CALDER WAS not a man prone to drinking alone, but he made an exception on his wedding day. Technically, he supposed, as he opened a second bottle of champagne, it was not his wedding day. Technically, it was the day his wedding was supposed to have been.

"To the bride!" he said, lifting the delicate wine flute in a mock salute before draining the champagne that had been purchased to toast the future of the happy couple. Growling in frustration, he hurled the empty glass against the brick fireplace and took smug satisfaction in the crash and tinkle of glass shattering against brick.

May she enjoy the same happiness she's always enjoyed with her ex-husband!

She'd slept with him, for God's sake! Her ex-husband. The ex-husband who'd gone into a rage and broken the windshield on Mike's car with a baseball bat the first time Mike had parked it in her driveway. The ex-husband against whom—on the advice of an attorney Mike had paid for—she'd filed a restraining order because he'd harassed her to the point of putting her job in jeopardy.

She was supposed to marry me within the week, and she gets lonely and sleeps with her ex-husband! The ex-husband who'd forgotten the kids' birthdays, not shown up for scheduled visits and moved across the country without a backward glance. The ex-husband who'd been so erratic with child support payments that Mike had to loan Beth Ann money to pay her electric bill.

The sound of the breaking glass aroused Dodger, Mike's aging chow-shepherd-setter, who rose stiffly and ambled over to investigate the carnage.

"Sit!" Mike ordered, before the dog could reach the broken glass. "I may be a veterinarian, but I'm in no mood to sew up mutt noses or tongues tonight."

No condition, either, he admitted as he pulled himself out of the recliner and stalked to the kitchen for the broom and dustpan. He went back into the living room, swept up the shards and dropped the demolished flute into the wastebasket. Then he took a liter beer stein, a souvenir from Oktoberfest, from the cabinet.

Much better, he decided, when he'd fit the better half of a bottle of champagne into the tankard. Now he could get down to some serious drinking without having to waste energy pouring and sipping and pouring and sipping. Damned sissy champagne flutes weren't made for a man's hands, anyway.

The mantel clock chimed the hour, taunting him with the realization that if things had worked out differently, he would have been leaving for a brief honeymoon right around this time.

"Prosit!" he toasted in the direction of the clock before taking a hearty gulp of wine.

If things were different! Yeah. Right. He chortled bitterly. *If.*

If he hadn't left Beth Ann on the other side of the country. *If* her son hadn't run away in the first place. *If* he'd gone to California to bring back the kid himself instead of buying a ticket for Beth Ann so she could do it.

If Beth Ann hadn't slept with her ex-husband. It always came down to that. The bottle of champagne he'd already downed did nothing to dim the memory of their conversation—the one they'd had when he'd surprised her at her ex-husband's apartment. It hadn't taken him long to leap to the obvious conclusion. Beth Ann wasn't able to look him in the eye and she spoke only in single-word sentences. It hadn't been much of a leap.

To her credit, Beth Ann hadn't tried to deny it when he'd confronted her.

She'd tried to explain, which was far worse.

"It just . . . it just happened," she'd said. "I was so upset—"

Of course she'd been upset! Most mothers *would* be upset when their ten-year-old son got angry over losing electronic-game privileges and hitchhiked across the country to live with his father. She'd been frantic with worry and her seven-year-old daughter had been hysterical.

"I was . . . I got here, and I was so . . . relieved to see Danny safe, and Steve was so understanding—"

Understanding? Her ex-husband? The jerk? Mike had been too shocked to point out that *he* had been understanding, too—understanding enough to drop over a thousand dollars for plane tickets so Beth Ann and her daughter could fly from Florida to California to bring the runaway home.

It would have been kinder if Beth Ann had just shut up at that point, but she'd kept explaining. Or trying to.

"He misses us," she'd said. "He says he's learned his lesson. When he had to give us up, he realized—"

Mike had to clench his jaw to keep from wailing at her gullibility. "He didn't *have* to give you and the kids up, Beth Ann. He gave you up voluntarily. He's the one who decided to skip his scheduled visits and default on his support payments. He's the one who decided he had to live on the opposite side of the continent."

"He's made mistakes—"

"How astute of you to notice."

Beth Ann frowned. "He says he's sorry."

"How touching."

"He and I were married twelve years, Mike."

"You and I are getting married Saturday, Beth Ann," Mike said sarcastically. "Doesn't that mean anything?"

Her face turned tragic. "Oh, Mike, I'm so confused."

"About us?"

"About—" She swallowed a threatening sob. "He wants us to stay here and try to make a go of it."

"You're not considering it?" Mike asked, amazed that he even had to ask. But as he gave voice to the question, he realized that she really *was* considering it.

"The kids are glad to see him. He *is* their father."

"The father of the year!" Mike muttered bitterly. He saw the anguish in Beth Ann's eyes. "You *are* considering it," he accused.

Beth Ann exhaled a dismal sigh. "He's been part of my life for as long as I can remember. We have a history."

"You and Steven have a history. You . . . and I . . . and the children," he said stiffly, measuring his words, "are supposed to have a future—beginning Saturday at two o'clock."

Beth Ann pressed her palms to her temples as if suffering from an excruciating headache. An odd, high-pitched sound came from her throat. "Oh, Mike!"

"I'm leaving for the airport in half an hour," Mike said crisply. "You and the kids can come with me, or you can stay here with the father of the year."

"Mike, please. Be fair."

Fair? he thought. He'd neutered her cat, spayed her dog, changed the brakes in her car, pruned her trees and cleaned her gutters. He'd held her hand through a visit to the emergency room with her daughter's broken arm and given her son the birds-and-bees-and-safe-sex talk. Hell, he'd even spoken to her daughter's class on Career Day. *While her ex-husband was forgetting to write support checks and skipping scheduled visits with the kids.*

"I've never been anything *but* fair to you."

"But you can't expect me to—"

"I didn't expect you to sleep with your ex-husband."

"I told you. That just . . . happened."

"Yeah. Well, the thing is, it happened—and less than a week before our wedding." Circling her wrists, he guided her hands away from her face and searched her eyes.

"Why?" he asked. "Why did you stay here? Why didn't you come back to Florida and tell me about it so we could work through it?"

"I was embarrassed," she said. "And confused."

"About whether you'd rather be on the West Coast with him or on the East Coast with me?"

"About...everything," she said with a sob. "Oh, Mike, I have to think—"

"If you have to think about it for more than five seconds, then you've already made your decision," Mike said.

Within hours, he was on a plane headed for home. Alone.

Now, abysmally alone, he was drinking champagne on what would have been his wedding day, and the numbness accompanying the shock of their abrupt breakup was slowly giving way to a miasmic blend of unpleasant emotions: anger over Beth Ann's infidelity; sadness over the loss of the closeness they'd shared; disappointment over his failure to make it work; self-loathing over having made the same old mistake again.

"This one's for you, Calder," he said, lifting the beer stein high. "To another outstanding job of proving that nice guys finish last."

He chugalugged the champagne and reached for another bottle, thinking, with tipsy logic, that it was a good thing the wedding was to have been a small, intimate celebration. Otherwise, he might end up drinking himself to death, instead of just into a stupor.

The phone rang while Mike was in the process of uncorking the bottle. Mike decided to let the answering machine pick up the call. If it was anything less than a plague threatening to wipe out the entire house cat population of America, it would have to wait until he was over the hangover he was working on.

"I don't know if I have the right person, but since your name is Mike—" The voice coming through the speaker was unfamiliar. An awkward pause ensued before the woman continued.

"I'm calling from California. My phone number is the same as yours except for the area code. I wasn't sure I should call, but I was so upset that my husband said I should try."

"Are you talking to one of those machines?" a male voice interjected from the background, only to be shushed by the frantic woman.

"We've been getting phone calls from a little girl named Shelly who keeps asking for Mike," the woman continued. "She insists this is his number."

The corkscrew was fully engaged, but instead of extracting the cork from the bottle, Mike froze, listening intently to the stranger's voice. Beth Ann's daughter's name was Shelly.

"I finally asked her where Mike lived and she said Orlando, so I looked up the area code. If you know this child, please call her. She sounds desperate to talk to you. And if you are the right Mike, I wish you'd let me know so I can quit worrying. I mean . . . this could be a crank caller, but it sounds—"

Uttering a blistering curse, Mike set the bottle aside, lunged for the phone, thanked the woman for calling and assured her he would get in touch with Shelly.

He cursed again as he hung up the receiver. Why the hell couldn't it have been something simple—like a plague threatening America's house cats? If he had to list the things he didn't want to do on this of all nights, talking to Beth Ann's daughter would go at the very top.

With a forlorn sigh, he reflected that the only thing more pathetic than a seven-year-old girl without a daddy was a thirty-eight-year-old veterinarian without a family. He and Shelly had been buddies from the moment they met. Mike had filled in for the father who'd disappeared from her life, and Shelly had occupied the space in Mike's heart that only a child could claim.

Up to the moment his taxi had arrived at Beth Ann's ex-husband's apartment, Mike had been hoping Beth Ann would come to her senses and agree to return to Florida with him. But it was Shelly who'd run to him, crying, for an urgent goodbye hug. The image of her pretty little face, contorted with grief over being abandoned once again, haunted him.

She'd been trying to call him.

Wearily, he looked up the number and dialed.

BETH ANN'S EX-HUSBAND answered the phone and summoned Beth Ann with a gruff growl. Mike was sure he meant for him to hear as he told Beth Ann in a scathingly sarcastic tone, "It's your *boyfriend.*"

"Mike?"

"Hello, Beth Ann."

"If you called hoping I'd be all nostalgic because of what day it is—after walking out on me the way you did—"

"I didn't call hoping anything," Mike said. If she'd had a change of heart, a sudden realization that she'd made a mistake by staying with her ex-husband, she'd have called him by now.

"Then why *did* you call?"

"To talk to Shelly."

"No way! We've just got her calmed down. I don't want her upset again."

"Calmed down?"

"It hasn't been a great day," she said caustically.

"She's been trying to call me," he said.

"What? No way. She hasn't even asked."

"She's been getting a woman with my number in your area code," he said patiently. "Please, Beth Ann. Maybe I can explain—"

Beth Ann's laugh was ugly. "Maybe you could explain to me."

"We'd have to explain to each other," Mike replied sadly, wishing it were possible. Wishing she could make him understand how she could have crawled into bed with her ex-husband after everything the jerk had done to her.

"Let me talk to Shelly," he said softly. "Please."

Her sigh of acquiescence slid through the phone lines. "I guess it can't hurt anything. Just . . . don't upset her, okay?"

"When did I ever upset her, Beth Ann?" He hadn't created the confusion that had plagued the child's life. He'd been prepared to step in and be the father she needed.

"I'll get her," Beth Ann said, leaving Mike holding the receiver to his ear, wondering how he was going to get through the upcoming conversation as he listened to vague noises of confusion and shuffling in the background.

"Hello." The little-girl voice was squeakier than usual.

"Hey, Silly, is that you?"

"It's *Shelly*," she corrected. She didn't giggle the way she usually did, but her voice gained strength as she fell into their old pattern of teasing.

"This is Mike."

"I know."

"I hear you wanted to talk to me."

"Uh-huh."

"What's on your mind, Silly?" *As if he didn't know.*

"Shelly!" she said with a weary sigh, as if the effort to keep up the game had overwhelmed her. But as she spoke again, it was outrage he heard in her voice. "Mommy forgot about the wedding. I tried to tell her it was today, but she wouldn't listen."

Mike searched frantically for a suitable response. Before he could come up with one, she continued. "I even showed her the calendar, and she still wouldn't listen. She made me go to my room. Only it's not my room. It's a silly old storage room with a sleeping roll on the floor. And she said there isn't going to be any wedding."

"She's right, honey."

"But—I was supposed to be flower girl, remember? I had a special dress and everything."

"I know. But sometimes—"

"Aren't you going to be my new daddy?"

"No, Shelly. I can't do that."

"But I wanted you to be my daddy," she said, her voice breaking.

"Oh, honey, I wanted that, too. But things between your mother and I just didn't work out."

"She said bad things about you after you left. I told her she wasn't being very nice, and she told me I was being disrespectful."

"You have to respect your mommy, Shelly. It's not easy being a grown-up. She was probably a little sad. Maybe you could be extra nice to her right now."

"But you were going to be my daddy."

"You already have a daddy."

"He's not nice like you are."

Mike closed his eyes and clenched the receiver in a death grip. Why didn't she just take a dull knife and dig out his heart with it? "Give him a chance. You haven't been around him in a long time.... Maybe he just needs to remember how to be a daddy."

He could hear her breathing on the other end of the line.

"I still love you, Shelly. We can be buddies, even if I can't be your daddy."

"Can I call you?"

"Why don't you write me letters? That way, you could send me pictures. And I'll write you letters back."

A sniff. "What about Lady and Tramp?" The stuffed animals he'd bought her on a trip to Walt Disney World had been "living" at his house for Shelly to visit when Beth Ann was visiting Mike.

"What if I sent them to you?" he suggested.

"In the mail?"

"Uh-huh."

"Wouldn't they be scared?"

"Naw! They'd have each other. It would be an adventure."

"Okay."

"When you get them, you can write me a note and tell me they got there safe and sound."

There was a commotion at the other end of the line. "I've got to go now," Shelly said, sounding vexed.

"All right. I'll be looking for a letter from you."

"Mike?" Beth Ann's voice.

"I'm going to send her Lady and Tramp."

"Thank you."

"I assume you'll still be there when they arrive." He wasn't even sure why he'd asked, especially in such a snide way. He was past hoping she might come to her senses and hurry back to him, begging for forgiveness and understanding and a fresh start. Somewhere between the Grand Canyon and the Mississippi River, he'd realized that she'd never really worked through her feelings for her ex-husband, and that he'd rushed into their relationship out of a yearning for roots and family instead of out of love for her. And Beth Ann...well, Beth Ann had been looking for a man she could count on.

"Why not?" she asked sharply. "Look, Mike, I told you I was considering staying in California." There was a strained silence. "Actually," she said finally, "I've been job hunting. You wouldn't believe how much higher salaries are here."

"I hope you find what you're looking for," Mike said. "I mean that."

"Thank you." She paused, then added hesitantly, "Mike—"

"Yeah," he said, relieved to hear the note of finality in the way she addressed him. "Me, too. Take care of the kids, huh? They're great kids."

"You're going to be a great father someday."

"Yeah. Right." *Nice shot, Beth Ann,* he thought as he replaced the receiver. She must have seen from the very beginning how much he wanted—needed—a family. And how vulnerable he was because of it. She'd played on that vulnerability as surely as he'd leapt at the opportunity to play the role of hero charging in to rescue the women and children from the bad guy.

The only problem was, the good guy didn't end up with the girl.

Mike went back to the champagne, gave the corkscrew a savage yank and scrambled to get the stein under the mouth of the bottle as the liquid spewed forth. This was one night he didn't want to waste a drop.

For a while he relished the sweetness of self-pity. He felt like hell, and no one could blame him. His fiancée had slept with her ex-husband and the child he'd grown to love like a daughter had been taken from him. Instead of becoming a family man, he'd become the cuckolded husband-to-be.

Husband-never-to-be was more like it! Husband-never-to-be, father-never-to-be, happy-never-to-be—

At some point during his consumption of the third bottle of champagne, Mike suddenly began to see his situation more clearly. It was as though a huge bank of lights had been turned on, illuminating truths that should have been obvious to him all along: he was a nice guy, and nice guys were fools. Clowns. Jesters in the court of courtship. Comic relief in the war of the sexes.

He was an anachronism, a fossil; the last dinosaur in the valley; the last cowboy wearing a white hat in a sea of black Stetsons; the last knight to don armor and go out to deliver maidens from peril.

Well, no more! he thought with drunken resolve. No one could be exploited unless he allowed himself to be. He was going to wise up and get tough. Get rid of his white hat. Put away his armor and quit rescuing damsels in distress.

He was going to join the rest of the hardened cynics in the real world. He was going to quit getting attached to fatherless waifs and desperate women. He was going to just swear off women altogether—

Swear off women?

Whoa! Stop the presses. Put on the brakes. What was he thinking? He didn't want to swear off women! He wasn't a monk. He was a healthy man in his prime and healthy men in their primes had needs, after all. He liked women. He liked the way they smelled, he liked the sound of their laughter and he liked the way they felt. Why should he give them up?

With the lucidity of logic that came from four bottles of champagne, he realized that he shouldn't have to give up women at all. He just needed to find a different type of woman. A woman who would like him without needing him so much, who could do as much for him as he could do for her. Someone who could appreciate him without exploiting him. A woman unencumbered by the past and anxious to embrace the future, who was not only his intellectual equal, but his financial and emotional equal, as well.

A new kind of woman. That was it. The answer. He would be more selective. Particular. Discriminating. He would set certain standards and abide by them. No more blundering into relationships based on chemistry. No more being seduced by a woman's needing him. No more getting attached to children who were no concern of his.

The longer he pondered the idea, the better he liked it. He hadn't rushed into setting up a clinic or buying a house without preparing a list of requirements and shopping around. Why would he be less careful in selecting a woman?

The plan was too profound to be committed entirely to memory, he concluded. He needed something tangible to remind him of his resolve. With Dodger padding after him, Mike walked to the kitchen and dug through his catchall drawer for a notepad. Under the letterhead imprinted with the name Smith's Worm Capsules, he wrote:

*Mike Calder's Minimum Requirements for a
Woman*

1. She will have a good job that pays well.

2. No children.

3. Doesn't believe men are a scourge upon the
earth—no abusive ex-husbands, stalking ex-lovers,
harassing bosses or any other troublesome man in
her past.

4. Drives a relatively new car still under war-
ranty and has an established rapport with a professional mechanic.

5. Lives in apartment or condo, or has a lawn
service under contract.

Pleased with his efforts, Mike read the list drunkenly
to Dodger, who responded with a canine cock of his head
and a soft whine.

"I know," Mike replied. "I *am* a genius. Nice of you to
say so." He skimmed the list again. "Just one last
thing—"

6. Sexy.

"There," he said, adding a final period with the dot of
his pen before returning his gaze to the dog. "A man has
to have *some* fun, doesn't he?"

MONDAY MORNING, Mike posted the list above the utility room sink at the clinic, where he would see it each time he washed his hands.

Suzie, his office manager, discovered it right away, as he'd known she would. Suzie always noticed everything. And Suzie always had an opinion. She responded to *Mike Calder's Minimum Requirements for a Woman* with a derisive snort. "Did a little soul-searching this weekend, did we?"

Mike responded with a frown.

Undaunted, Suzie perused him with the sharp gaze developed during the raising of three sons. "You must have also done a little drinking. You don't look as pretty as you usually do."

"There was all that champagne," Mike said, unfazed by her upbraiding. "I couldn't let it go to waste."

Suzie's "harrumph" was like that of an impatient parent. "I knew it was a mistake for you to hole up by yourself. You should have been with people, gone out and had some fun." She lifted the glasses hanging from a chain around her neck and put them on. Her forehead wrinkled with concentration as she gave the list a careful reading.

"I wasn't in a partying mood," Mike said dryly.

Suzie parked her glasses on the very tip of her nose and looked at Mike across the rim. "So you're looking for a 'rich bitch' now."

"I'm looking for an economic and emotional equal," he corrected.

Suzie removed her glasses and let them fall to the end of the chain on her ample chest. "Seems a bit . . . *extreme* to me."

"From now on," Mike said firmly, "when I go out with a woman, I'm going to be more to her than a hunk of muscle and a checkbook."

"Uh-huh."

"I mean it, Suzie. I've been too easy too long. I'm tired of doing women's yard work and fixing their cars and fending off their ex-husbands, then having them run off with the first jerk who comes along."

"You've had some bad breaks," Suzie conceded.

"Some? They should stamp Sucker across my forehead, the way they used to brand thieves."

Suzie shrugged. "Whatever. It's your love life. But you still seem like a yard-work-and-car-repair kind of guy to me."

"That was the *old* Mike Calder."

"Well, if you're serious about this, you ought to be real interested in seeing the letter that came when you were in California. It's from Samantha Curry."

"Samantha Curry? Should I know the name?"

Suzie rolled her eyes. "Men! Don't you read anything but the front page and the sports section? Just Samantha Curry of *the* Orlando Currys. She's a socialite and a sort of professional volunteer do-gooder. She's organizing one of those community rabies vaccination days and she wants you to man a clinic at one of the neighborhood shopping centers."

"You think she meets my requirements?"

"She's beautiful, single and rich."

"No kids? No ex-husbands?"

"Just all that money and all those degrees from all the right schools."

"Then maybe I ought to man a clinic. Send the form back to her and write the times on my calendar."

"I'll put you down for supplying a carton of vaccine, too."

"That's very civic-minded of me."

"You want to make a good impression, don't you?"

"Yes. And this time it's tax deductible—unlike the tennis shoes I bought for Beth Ann's son, and the lawyer's fees I paid for Beth Ann, and the down payment I made on the braces for what's-her-name's daughter year before last, and . . . I could go on, but I won't."

Suzie placed her hand gently on Mike's shoulder. "Let go of it, Mike. You're a nice guy. That's nothing to be ashamed of."

"I don't mind being nice, but I'm through being easy," Mike said. "Women with sob stories can just find some other poor sucker to tell them to. Sob stories aren't going to cut it anymore. Not with this guy!"

2

ANGELINA WINTERS looked at her daughter's face and experienced the frustrating helplessness of motherhood. Lily's features were delicate, but the somber expression in her large green eyes revealed a seriousness uncommon to seven-year-olds.

"See," the child argued, pointing to the newspaper. "Puppies are not too 'spensive. They're free."

Angelina exhaled a weary, languid sigh. Whose bright idea was it to teach second-graders to read the want ads, anyway? "It's not the puppy that's expensive, Lily. It's everything the puppies need. They need food—"

"Puppies are little, Mommy. They don't eat much."

"They also need—" Why could she suddenly not think of a single expensive thing that puppies needed? She should have been prepared for this battle; she and Lily had been engaged in the war for over a week—ever since the guidance counselor at Lily's school had suggested the little girl might benefit from the company of a pet.

"Flea spray," Angelina continued, "and collars and leashes and shots and—" She stopped short at the stricken expression in Lily's large green eyes. "Lily?"

"I know why we can't have a puppy," Lily said. "It's because we don't have a good home!"

"A good home? Lily, what do you mean? Of course we have—"

"The paper says, 'Free to a good home,' and we don't have a good home because we don't have a daddy."

Scooping her daughter into her arms, Angelina hugged her tightly and rocked her back and forth, wishing she could absorb the child's misery and insecurities like a sponge. "We've talked about this before, sweetheart. I love you, and you love me, don't you?"

Lily nodded silently against Angelina's chest.

"Well, as long as we love each other, we have a very good home."

Lily's head popped up. "Then we can get a puppy free."

Angelina didn't know whether to laugh or cry. She wasn't quite sure that she hadn't just been conned in a most calculating manner, but she was certain of one thing: she'd lost the war. The prospect of getting a puppy had wrought a miraculous transformation in her daughter.

"There's a telephone number in the ads," Lily said helpfully.

Again Angelina looked at her daughter. "You're *sure* you don't want a hamster or a parakeet?"

"I want a puppy!" Lily insisted.

Napoleon and Waterloo, Custer and the Little Big Horn, Angelina and the Weekend Want Ads—

"Well, in that case," Angelina said, "you can dial, and I'll do the talking."

Angelina held the receiver to her ear, guiltily hoping that the line would be busy, or that no one would answer, or that she would be politely informed that all the puppies had found new homes—anything that would give her a reprieve. If she could only get Lily into a pet store long enough, she was convinced the child would eventually fall in love with a lop-eared rabbit or a guinea pig.

Angelina didn't have anything against dogs. She loved dogs. She also knew how expensive they were and how much trouble they were to train—just as she knew how thinly her monthly salary was already stretched and how little time and energy she had left after juggling single parenthood, a full-time job and single-handedly keeping up a house with three bedrooms, two baths and a semitropical lawn.

But she was just plain out of luck. A woman who identified herself as Kaitlin O'Quinn answered on the second ring, and cheerfully informed her that there were three puppies available, and that she'd reserved the morning to interview prospective owners. Angelina found herself writing down directions to the woman's apartment and telling her that she and Lily would be there within the hour.

If Lily hadn't been anchored by a seat belt, Angelina thought a few minutes later, she'd probably squirm right out of the car. Angelina hadn't seen her daughter as excited about anything in the twenty months since Thomas had moved out of the house—twenty months of angst and upheaval surrounding a legal separation, a divorce with fights over division of the property and child support.

Devastated by the shake-up in her previously secure little world, Lily had not adjusted well to her parents' divorce. Then, just when Angelina was making progress with her, Thomas had dropped the bombshell that he was remarrying and acquiring two stepchildren. Lily had become more distraught and confused than ever when she realized that while her father had chosen to abandon her, he now had two strange children living with him. Her performance at school had dropped to the extent that she was in danger of having to repeat second grade.

It was her science teacher who'd noticed Lily's fascination with animals and her rapport with the various small critters who lived in aquariums in the science classroom. The teacher had conferred with the guidance counselor, who'd suggested to Angelina that Lily might respond to a pet.

Oh, why hadn't she gone to the pet store and surprised Lily with a fuzzy little bunny! Angelina thought. *But no. She'd wanted to be supermother. She'd wanted to involve Lily in the pet-selection process.* She'd envisioned an idyllic trip to the pet store and a jubilant Lily leaving with a cardboard box containing something small and simple and beloved.

Which only proved that mothers should think less and act more, she thought wryly while Lily chatted on and on about what she hoped the puppies would look like.

From the first mention of the word *pet,* Lily had been adamant that she wanted a puppy. Now Angelina was torn between logic and love for her daughter. A puppy meant vet bills and chewed-up shoes and fleas in the house and months of cleaning up puppy puddles on the carpet. But if a puppy could produce that uninhibited smile and that sparkle of excitement in her daughter's eyes . . .

Kaitlin O'Quinn had given excellent directions, and Angelina located the woman's apartment easily. Lily dashed ahead of her up the short walk to ring the doorbell and literally danced in place as they waited for someone to answer.

They could hear barking inside. Lily looked up at her mother with a beatific expression on her face. "Oh, Mommy!"

Oh, Mommy! Such a simple phrase to hold all the awe and wonderment of childhood, the joy of boundless hope and untethered anticipation that had been missing from Lily's life for too long. Such a simple phrase to melt a mother's heart.

Looking at her daughter's face, Angelina vowed that Lily would have her puppy. They'd been making it on her salary and Thomas's child support for a year and a half. They'd keep on making it—even with a dog.

The door opened and a young woman in jeans and a chambray shirt welcomed them. By the time Angelina had taken Kaitlin O'Quinn's proffered hand and introduced herself, Lily was already inside, giggling as she was assailed by three puppies. The mother dog sat nearby looking slightly bored, but surreptitiously casting a watchful eye over her brood. Angelina gestured toward her daughter and said, "My daughter, Lily."

"Lily," Kaitlin said, kneeling as she addressed the child. "I see you've already met the puppies."

The littlest of the litter, a long-haired, brown-spotted pup, leapt at Lily's knee, expecting attention. Lily picked it up and nestled it in her arms. "Are they boys or girls?"

At that moment one of the pups, a brown shorthair with a bulky body, barked at her. Lily's face registered surprise, then amusement at the dog's bravado.

"That one's a boy," Kaitlin said. "You can tell, can't you?"

"Yeah," Lily agreed with a giggle.

"This one's a boy, too," Kaitlin said, petting the third. "And the one you're holding is a girl."

"I want this one, Mommy," Lily said. "I want the girl."

"Are you sure?" Angelina asked, noting the female puppy's long hair with dismay. "Wouldn't you rather have the one who barked at you?" *The one with short hair.*

"No. He's too mean. This one likes me."

And will require spaying, Angelina thought. She turned to Kaitlin and gave a resigned shrug of her shoulders. "Looks like it's a done deal."

"Not quite so fast," Kaitlin said. She looked from Lily to Angelina and back. "These puppies are very special to me. I have to know that they're going to a good home."

Angelina saw the panic that crossed Lily's face and, suddenly, taking home that long-haired little female seemed the most important thing in the world. Every drop of her maternal instinct told her that Lily needed that puppy, needed it as surely as she needed food and shelter and hugs and loving discipline.

"Lily and I have talked this over," Angelina said. "She wants a puppy very badly, and we're prepared to take care of one."

Kaitlin gave Lily a firm look. "Puppies need lots of love. Can you give her that?"

Angelina had seldom seen Lily so serious as when she nodded in response. She was hugging the puppy as though afraid someone might wrest it from her. Yet, Angelina thought, it was a benign seriousness, not the youth-robbing seriousness she'd so often seen in her daughter's face.

"I'll love Princess. I'll play with her, too," Lily said meekly.

"Saints preserve us, she's named her already," Kaitlin said with a chuckle before directing her attention to Angelina. "Do you understand how much a puppy demands?"

"Oh, yes," Angelina said. "Believe me, I know. But Lily wants a dog and her teachers think it'll be good for her. We have a house, and a screened patio where the puppy can stay during the day."

"All right, then," Kaitlin said. "But you've got to promise to take my address and send me pictures of...*Princess* from time to time, so I'll know she's healthy and happy. She'll need her next shots in another two weeks."

Great! Angelina thought. *They'll probably only cost a million dollars each.*

"What kind of dog is Princess?" Lily asked on the way home.

"I'd say she has a little cocker spaniel, a little springer spaniel and a lot of fence jumper in her," Angelina speculated.

"Is that a good kind?"

"The best," Angelina assured her.

MIKE LOOKED OVER the head of his patient at the concerned pet owner. "Agatha's not ill, Mrs. Anderson," he said. "She's just obese."

"Agatha's not . . . *obese*," Mrs. Anderson replied with an offended air. "Her fur just sticks out."

Mike grinned. "The scale doesn't lie, Mrs. Anderson. I'm afraid that long hair is hiding a bit of blubber. I'm going to recommend special food for her, and I want you to measure the portions every day. You should notice a difference in her energy level within a couple of weeks. And no people food."

"Not even tuna?" Mrs. Anderson asked, her chin quivering as she cast a sympathetic look at her pampered gray Persian. "Agatha loves tuna."

"Not even water-packed tuna," Mike told her sternly. "The mercury in the tuna tends to make cats lethargic, even if Agatha could handle the calories—which she can't."

"Poor Agatha," Mrs. Anderson cooed as she scooped the stocky cat into her arms. "Is the mean old doctor putting you on a diet?"

"The mean old doctor is trying to make sure Agatha enjoys every one of her nine lives," Mike said drolly. Leaning out the door of the examining room, he called for Suzie.

"Whatcha need, Doc?"

"Give Mrs. Anderson a starter sample of Svelte Cat for Agatha, please."

"Sure thing, Doc," Suzie said, reaching out to give Agatha a pat. "Watching your waistline, eh, Agatha?"

Turning, she opened the door to the supply closet, and told Mike, over her shoulder, "Your last patient's waiting in room two."

"I live to serve," Mike mumbled, hoping his last case of the day didn't involve any complicated procedures. He was already running ten minutes past his normal closing time. With a final nod to Mrs. Anderson, he lumbered into the next examination room.

His first impression was that the room was empty. Then he spied the child sitting in the plastic chair on the far side of the stainless steel examining table, a beautiful little girl with large green eyes and dark curly hair. She was clutching a spotted puppy to her chest.

"Hello," he said as genially as possible, hoping to put the girl at ease.

The greeting was met with a subtle hunching of the shoulders and a wary, tight-lipped expression. Picking up the file card Suzie had left on the corner of the counter,

Mike scanned it briefly, then knelt next to the child. "Is this Princess?" he asked softly.

Eyeing him distrustfully, the girl hugged the puppy tighter. "Uh-huh."

The seriousness in the set of the child's cherubic features made Mike want to pull the frightened child into his arms and comfort her, but he didn't want to risk frightening her even more. If she started screaming, he'd find himself faced with a mother convinced her 'little darling' had fallen into the clutches of a child molester.

He saw her throat convulse as she swallowed before asking, "Are you going to give my puppy a shot?"

Mike had to bite his tongue to keep from chuckling. So that was at the bottom of all that angst. "I'm afraid so, sweetheart." He risked a tentative smile. "You wouldn't want your puppy to get sick, would you?"

She shook her head solemnly.

"What's your name?" he asked, petting the dog, hoping to establish a rapport with both animal and owner.

"Lily."

"Well, Lily, my name's Dr. Mike Calder. You can call me Dr. Mike."

Lily gave a grudging half nod.

"I've got to give Princess her checkup now," he said, easing the dog from her arms. She let him take the puppy, but watched him guardedly.

"Maybe you could stand next to the table and keep her calm while I'm examining her," he suggested.

"Okay," she said, moving to the table's edge where she could reach her puppy.

"I'm going to look at Princess's eyes and ears," Mike said, switching on his flashlightlike scope. "This doesn't hurt at all." He examined one ear, then rotated the dog's head so he could see the other one. "I'll bet your doctor does this when you go to see him, doesn't he?"

"Uh-huh," Lily agreed. "But my doctor's a lady, not a man."

Mike feigned a surprised expression. "A lady! Are you sure? I didn't know girls could be doctors."

Catching his playful tone, Lily giggled. "Yes."

Mike sheathed a thermometer in a sterile plastic casing and lubricated it. "I'm going to take Princess's temperature now."

"Why do you have all that gooey stuff on the thermometer? Won't it taste yukky?"

Mike smiled, thinking that Lily was going to *love* what happened next. Kids always did.

"Dogs can't hold thermometers in their mouths," he explained. "They bite them and break them. I need her other end."

He watched Lily's jaw drop in disbelief as he lifted the dog's tail and inserted the thermometer.

"I'm going to tell my mother what you did!" she snapped, outraged, as soon as she'd recovered enough from the surprise to speak.

"I'll bet your doctor or your mommy took your temperature this way when you were a baby," he said calmly.

Lily shook her head. "Uh-uh."

Mike grinned. "Ask her."

After a silent moment, he removed the thermometer and read it. "Just right. You must take very good care of Princess. She's a very healthy puppy."

"Uh-huh," Lily agreed, apparently over her shock.

"Is your mother out in the waiting room?" he asked as he palpated the dog's abdomen. The next thing on the agenda was the s-h-o-t, and he thought it might be less traumatic to the child, the dog—and not least of all, the veterinarian—if he did not have to vaccinate the puppy in front of the child.

Lily sighed. "She came in to fill out all the papers, but then she had to go back and fix the tire."

Mike didn't get a good feeling from that little revelation. Knowing he shouldn't ask, he nevertheless did. "What tire?"

"The tire on the car," she said. "It was flat."

A woman in his parking lot changing a tire. That was great. Just great. A damsel in distress. He made a concerted effort to squelch the urge to rescue her, reminding himself that he had sworn off the role of knight-errant. His days of slaying dragons and banishing villains were over—along with his habit of being suckered in by needy females. He'd made a promise to himself, and he was going to stick to it.

"Is your daddy working on the tire with her?" he asked hopefully.

"We don't have a daddy anymore." The pain that crossed the child's face as she spoke ripped at his heart. He'd seen *that* look all too often. Always before, it had been his cue to dash into the role of substitute papa—just as he had with Shelly.

And look where it got you—and where it left Shelly, he thought, recalling with a pang of regret the heart-rending letter he'd received from the child who felt abandoned and betrayed. It read:

Dear Mike

Lady and Tramp got here just fine, but they're sad because they'd rather be at your house. I wish they still lived there so I could visit them again.

Love, Shelly

Mike forced himself back to the present. "Have you ever had a shot?" he asked as he filled the syringe.

The child's, "Uh-huh" was almost a whisper.

He turned around slowly. "Then you know that it only hurts for a second or two. No longer than it takes to say Tippecanoe. Can you say Tippecanoe?"

Lily repeated the word.

"Excellent," Mike said. "Now I want you to say it again as I give Princess her shot, and by the time you've said it, the whole thing will be over. Ready?"

Lily's chin quivered as she nodded.

"Okay. Now close your eyes and say the magic word."

Lily squeezed her eyes shut and grimaced. "Tippe-canoe," she said through clenched teeth.

Mike did the dastardly deed. Princess gave a token yelp, and Lily's eyes flew open. By that time, though, Mike was removing the needle. "All done," he announced with a reassuring smile. "Princess gets a puppy cookie for being a good doggie. Do you want to give it to her?"

Lily nodded, took the biscuit he offered her and fed it to the dog.

"We're all finished here," Mike said, scooping up Princess and handing her to Lily. "You can go back to the waiting room and talk to Suzie while I go see if your mommy needs any help with that tire."

A flat tire, he told himself. That's all it was. No more. No less. Simple courtesy dictated that he offer to help. The apprehension raising prickles on the back of his neck was an overreaction. He had no reason to worry. So the waif's mom had no man to fix her flat tire. So what? He was worrying about phantoms. After all, he hadn't even seen the woman. She was probably leaning against the front fender of her Mercedes or BMW, waiting for the auto club man.

Even if he were willing to let himself get pulled into a . . . *situation*—which he wasn't—she probably wasn't even his type. She was probably as homely as a bar of soap—

With a daughter who looked like a cherub? No way, Calder. No, a worm of intuition told him she was not going to be homely, and past experience told him she was not going to be leaning against the fender of a Mercedes or BMW.

He steeled himself for the inevitable and opened the door. The sun blinded him as he stepped outside and he paused a moment, squinting, while his eyes adjusted to the brightness.

It was not difficult to pick out Mrs. Winters's car; his van and Suzie's hulking Buick were the only two other vehicles in the small lot. Mrs. Winters's car was not a Mercedes. It was not a BMW. It was an aging domestic compact.

Mrs. Winters was too engrossed in loosening lug nuts to notice him. Although his vantage point did not allow him to see her face, he surmised immediately that Mrs. Winters was not homely.

It's a test, he thought, taking in the rich, dark hair curling in profusion at the top of the collar of a white, slightly sheer blouse, through which he could see the vaguest impression of some lacy little underthing with narrow straps. *Fate was testing him.*

The blouse was tucked into a dark gray skirt that hugged voluptuous hips. A wide black belt separated the two pieces, defining a narrow waist.

Her shoulders vibrated with a sigh as she raised her right arm to wipe her forehead with the back of her wrist.

Resolving anew to remain uninvolved with this woman in any way beyond offering to help with the tire, he strode over to her and cleared his throat. "Mrs. Winters?"

She cocked her head back to look up at him curiously. *Oh, yes,* he thought. *He was definitely being tested.* Her dark brown eyes were large and expressive, her face oval, her mouth—

He forced himself not to dwell on her mouth. "I'm Dr. Calder. I just met your daughter and your puppy. Lily told me about the tire. Maybe I could give you a hand."

Lace-armored breasts rose beneath the soft folds of her blouse as she drew in a deep breath. "You don't have to— I couldn't impose—"

"Don't be silly," he said, kneeling beside her and grinning charmingly as he divested her of the wrench. "Despite the current frenzy for political correctness, there are still situations where brawn triumphs over brains."

"The screws *are* on really tight," she conceded.

You're telling me, sweetheart! Mike thought. But he said, "I'll see what I can do—as soon as I put something behind those back wheels."

"Oh?" Her mouth formed a perfect oval, framed by full lips.

Mike swallowed. "I've got some two-by-fours in my van."

He fetched the boards and wedged them beneath the good tires although, he observed, in this case the term *good* was relative. It did not mean good so much as not flat. Either she didn't know she needed tires, which was scary, or she couldn't afford them, which was worse.

Needy women! he thought, using the exertion of loosening the lug nuts as an outlet for his frustration.

"Do you have a jack?" he asked.

She nodded. "Uh-huh. I...it's under the... whatchamacallit. Like the illustration shows."

A whatchamacallit? It was a good thing he'd sworn off helpless women, Mike mused, because this one was *truly* helpless. The whatchamacallit! He got the jack, then squared it and pumped it up. *She would have probably been crushed under the car when she worked the wheel off—that is, of course, in the rare event that she'd ever managed to get the lug nuts loosened.*

"What made it go flat?" she asked as he rolled the tire aside. "Can you tell?"

Aside from the fact that it was worn-out? he thought uncharitably. Still, he rolled it slowly, examining what was left of the shallow treads. "Here it is," he said, pointing out a circle of metal. "Classic case. You picked up a nail."

She bent at the waist to examine the nail head, giving him an eye-level view of stockings shredded from the knee down, great calves, nice ankles, standard black pumps. "Just leave it in there," she said. "The last time it happened, the man at the filling station fussed at me for taking it out because it made it harder to find the hole."

He could *smell* her. Her cologne or whatever it was she wore was delicate and floral. Had he not been so close to her, and had it not been so warm, he probably would not have noticed it at all.

"You're not planning on patching it, are you?" he asked incredulously, trying to ignore that subtle scent. There was a smudge of tire black on her forehead, her wispy bangs had coiled damply and her cheeks were slightly flushed from the heat.

"What do you mean?" she asked. "Of course I have to fix it. The spare is one of those little temporary things."

"How long has it been since you had one patched?"

She sniffed impatiently. "A year, I guess. Maybe closer to a year and a half. It was right after—" She stiffened suddenly. "A year and a half. Why?"

"Because your tire might have been worth patching a year and a half ago, but it's almost bald now. You really should replace it."

"I need a new one?"

"You need *four* new ones."

He watched the information sink in, weighting her shoulders, bringing the wet brightness of threatening tears to her big brown eyes, bullying her fabulous mouth into a frown. "I need new tires?" she asked, as though hoping she'd misunderstood the first time.

"These are a hazard. They're almost bald. You're lucky you haven't had a blowout by now."

"Great!" she said, her calm snapping. "Oh, that's just great! Last month it was the fuel pump, and the mechanic said I need something called struts, and now you tell me the tires are worn-out."

Mike shrugged. "Don't shoot me. I'm only the messenger."

Mrs. Winters sighed dismally. "I'm sorry. It's just—"

Don't cry! Mike thought desperately, fearing that it was a real possibility. *Please don't cry!* Desperation was written on every one of her features. Her *very pleasing, female* features.

He felt himself slipping, sliding into the same old trap, wanting to comfort her, wanting to take care of her, wanting to wipe the tire black from her forehead and tease away her frown with nibbling kisses of reassurance.

You don't even know her first name! he chided himself.

"You . . . uh, you could probably get by with just replacing the front ones for now," he said, forcing himself to concentrate on aligning the holes of the spare with the lug nuts, "but I wouldn't hold off too long on the rear ones if I were you."

"They're really that bad?" she asked, staring at her filthy hands.

" 'Fraid so," he said. "There's a rest room inside where you can wash your hands," he offered. "I'll just finish up here and toss your tire in the trunk."

"Thank you for helping," she said. "I—"

"Brawn over brains, remember?" he said, grinning, hoping that she didn't think he was flirting.

Hoping that he wasn't flirting.

"But—"

"It was nothing, really. I'm just sorry about your tires—" *About your tires, your aging car, your money troubles, that your little girl doesn't have a daddy—*

Most of all, he was sorry that he wanted so badly to take care of her when he knew how disastrous it would be if he tried.

Watching her walk away, he admired the female quality of her movements even as relief swept over him that she was leaving. Anxious to avoid any chance of encountering her or her fatherless waif, he reentered the clinic from the back entrance.

Mike Calder's Minimum Requirements for a Woman stared him in the face as he scrubbed the grit from Mrs. Winters's tires from his hands, and he was damned glad of it. For a while there, he'd almost weakened.

He allowed himself a moment of gloating triumph as he realized how sorely he'd been tested—and that he'd passed with flying colors. He'd given Mrs. Winters a helping hand, but he hadn't even asked what her first name was.

3

"CAN YOU take a phone call?"

Mike, drying his hands, looked up at Suzie with a scowl of frustration. After the unsettling confrontation with the appealing but oh-so-wrong-for-him Mrs. Winters, he was in no mood for a closing-hour crisis. "Not unless a life hangs in the balance."

Shrugging his churlishness into insignificance, Suzie outscowled him. "It's *Ms. Curry.*"

"Ms. who?" Mike asked absently, tossing the paper towel into the waste can.

Suzie rolled her eyes. "How quickly we forget. Samantha Curry—*rich, beautiful* Samantha Curry who's organizing the community rabies vaccination clinics. I imagine that's what she's calling about."

"I'll take it in my office," Mike said, with the enthusiasm of a sloth.

"I wouldn't keep her waiting too long if I were you," Suzie said. "You're trying to make a good impression, remember?"

The button on his phone was winking like a roadhouse sign as Mike settled at his desk. He vented frustration with a powerful exhalation of breath before lifting the receiver, pressing the button and identifying himself.

"Dr. Calder? Samantha Curry. Thank you for taking a call so late in the day," purred a beautifully modulated female voice.

Mike's spirits lifted appreciably. Maybe the call was *just* what he needed to take his mind off Mrs. Winters and her bald tires and her big-eyed daughter. "No problem," he said. "I was just getting ready to lock up."

"I wanted to run the details of the vaccination day past you, but first, let me say how much I appreciate your volunteering to man one of our stations."

Mike had saved the lives of nearly dead pets and not heard as much gratitude in the voices of their owners as he heard in hers. "It's my pleasure," he said magnanimously. Then, for good measure, he added, "After all, rabies vaccination is important."

"I've assigned you to the Palm Isle Shopping Center. Our volunteers will be setting up on the sidewalk near the cinema. It's not far from your clinic. Do you know where it is?"

"Yes."

"Our volunteers will do the paperwork and put tags on collars, so all you have to do is show up and start shooting."

She paused, and Mike, hearing her intake of breath, imagined a female chest rising. Mrs. Winters's appealing female chest, to be exact.

Damn it!

"Dr. Calder?" The purr of his name through the receiver snapped him back to the conversation.

"Just show up and start shooting," he said amiably. "It sounds simple enough."

"I'm going to put the details in a letter, but if you have any questions at all, please don't hesitate to call."

"I won't," he said, suddenly firmly convinced that he'd have at least one question that would necessitate his getting in touch with the sultry voice on the other end of the line.

"Great. And thanks again for agreeing to give up your Saturday for us. We need to get these pets protected, and I know we're going to have a great turnout."

"I hope so."

"If I don't talk to you again, I'll see you next month."

"You will?"

"Yes. I'll be making the circuit from site to site throughout the day so I can thank our volunteers in person."

"I'll look forward to meeting you, then," Mike said quite sincerely. If there was anything to be learned from his encounter with Mrs. Winters, it was that he was far overdue for a little male-female interaction.

Man was not created to be solitary—or celibate.

With that thought in mind, he went into the boarding room to check on the animals who were spending the night at the clinic. The postop patients were drowsy, but none showed any sign of infection, and his only other boarding patient, an aging collie, was showing signs of improvement. He was giving the collie a little extra attention when he heard Suzie's voice, muffled by the walls that separated the boarding room from the reception area.

Hoping no emergency had cropped up to prolong his workday yet again, Mike went to the reception area to check it out and arrived just in time to see Suzie hang up the phone.

"Any problem?" he asked.

"Just seeing if Inez is ready for bingo night."

"It *is* Thursday, isn't it?" Mike said. Suzie took her mother-in-law to play bingo every Thursday. "Is Inez all charged up for a big game?"

"She's raring to go. She found a new button for her jackpot hat, and she's convinced it's lucky." Suzie put a plastic cover over the computer keyboard and took her purse from the bottom drawer of the desk. "By the way, Mrs. Winters said to tell you thank you for helping with the tire."

"All in a day's work," Mike said.

"She's a nice lady," Suzie said.

"Hmm," Mike agreed cautiously. Suzie was using her up-to-something tone of voice.

"Pretty, too."

"I didn't really notice." *Much.*

"Hmmph!"

"I was changing a tire!"

"Uh-huh." She paused. "She's divorced, you know."

"Yes, Suzie," Mike said. "Divorced, with a fatherless waif and bill collectors at the door."

"Her little girl was adorable."

"Hmm."

"She sure was proud of that puppy."

"Yes. She was."

"Too bad."

Mike knew he'd be sorry for swallowing the bait, but he knew Suzie well enough to know that if he didn't snap at it, she'd cram it down his throat. "*What's* too bad?"

"She left her backpack with her schoolbooks in the reception area."

"She'll be back for them tomorrow."

"Yeah," Suzie said with a meaningful sigh. "It's just—"

"Out with it, Suzie. What's your point?"

Suzie tilted her head sheepishly. "One of the books looks like a speller, and tomorrow's Friday."

"So?"

"Don't you remember elementary school? Friday is test day. She probably needs her book to study her words."

"If she's a good student, she probably knows them already. And if she's not a good student, she probably wouldn't learn them, anyway."

"Well, that's a fine attitude."

"I can't help it if she forgot her book the night before her spelling test."

Suzie frowned. "Maybe not, but—"

"But what?" Mike growled.

"If I didn't have to pick up Inez for bingo, I'd drop her backpack by their house. But it's in the opposite direction."

Mike realized where the conversation was headed. "Which means it's in the direction I'll be going."

"It's just a few blocks away. I checked. It wouldn't take you five minutes to detour and drop off the backpack."

A few blocks out of his way. It seemed simple enough—until Mike remembered Mrs. Winters's figure. And her bald tires. And her big-eyed waif of a kid. And his resolve not to play the knight to women with great cleavage, bald tires and waifish children.

"I don't do house calls," he said.

"We're not talking about performing major surgery," Suzie said. "You'd just be doing a good deed."

"I've already earned enough merit badges for two lifetimes," Mike said. *And I have the emotional scars to prove it.*

"Okay, I'll take them!" Suzie said sharply.

"You'll be late to bingo!"

"Yes. And Inez will get in a royal snit because she won't get a lucky seat, but—"

"Fine, I'll take the damn books to the kid!" Mike said.

"I drew a little map when I looked up the address," Suzie said, cagily picking up a piece of notepaper from the counter and handing it to him.

"Have I fired you lately?"

"Not this week," Suzie replied evenly. "But there's one more day left— Think you can find it?"

Mike shrugged. "Like you said, it's just a few blocks away."

Suzie turned serious suddenly. "All you have to do is ring the doorbell and give whoever answers the door the books."

"Her tires were bald," Mike said absently. "I tell you, Suzie, I feel guilty charging a woman like that just to look at a puppy and give it a shot."

"You don't have to lose too much sleep over it," Suzie said. "She got the 'new puppy special.'"

"New puppy special?"

"Basic puppy exam and shots, five bucks," Suzie replied wryly.

"Five bucks?" he exclaimed incredulously, but his mouth twitched with a smile that grew into a laugh. *New puppy special! Leave it to Suzie!*

"WHO WAS AT THE DOOR, Lily?" Angelina asked, hearing Lily enter the kitchen.

"Princess's doctor," Lily said.

Distracted by the cream sauce she was stirring, Angelina was slow absorbing what Lily had said. When the information clicked, she spun around. "Princess's—"

The rest of the question ended in an inhaled shriek as she discovered Dr. Calder standing not five feet away. He shrugged apologetically and held up Lily's backpack. "She forgot her books. My office manager thought she might need them, and . . . well, Lily had her hands full when she came to the door."

The veterinarian was in her kitchen! Angelina couldn't believe it. She was barefoot, and she was wearing a T-shirt that said, If You're Rich, I'm Available, over a pair of hopelessly faded shorts. The cereal bowls from breakfast were still in the sink and the veterinarian was in her kitchen.

The drop-dead handsome veterinarian who'd changed her tire for her. "I—" She broke off, too tongue-tied and addled by his unexpected presence to speak coherently. "I was stirring the sauce and...*the sauce!*" Whirling, she lifted the saucepan from the burner and stirred frantically before the sauce scorched or turned lumpy.

Having averted tragedy—or at least tragedy with the sauce—she replaced the pan, sprinkled a layer of shredded cheese atop the mixture and resumed stirring. Gently.

"Sorry about that," she said, stepping to the side of the stove so she could see him as she worked.

"That . . . uh, looks complicated," he observed. "You must be a gourmet."

"A gourmet?" She laughed, a bit nervously. "It's just cream sauce. It's not complicated, but you have to stir . . . you can't leave it . . . untended. That's why I couldn't answer the door."

"It smells delicious," he said.

"That's the cheese melting," she said. *Scintillating conversation, Angelina. Why don't you give him the whole recipe and really impress him! He's only a vet—* And he was still holding Lily's books.

"Lily," she said sharply. "Put Princess down and take your backpack from Dr.—" *Holy cow! She couldn't remember his name! Dr....Dr....Doc—* "Calder!" she said, hoping he hadn't noticed the long hesitation.

Refocusing her attention on Lily and the issue at hand, she asked, "Why are you carrying Princess around, anyway?"

"She tried to run out the door, so I had to hold her," Lily said matter-of-factly.

"We wouldn't want a nice dog like Princess getting lost," Dr. Calder said.

"Well, she's not going to get lost in the house," Angelina said. "Lily, put her down and take your books."

Lily exhaled an aggrieved sigh and gently set the puppy on the floor.

"Wasn't it nice of Dr. Calder to bring your books to you?" Angelina said.

"Uh-huh," Lily said, taking the backpack from him.

Angelina held her breath, hoping that Lily would thank him without additional prompting, and released it when Lily said politely, "Thank you for bringing my books."

"This is the last of the cheese," Angelina said, sprinkling the grated cheese into the pan. "I'll walk you to the door as soon as it's melted."

"No hurry," Doctor Calder said. Crossing his arms, he leaned against the counter casually. *Familiarly.*

Something changed at that moment. Something fundamental. Something elemental. Something . . . *electrical.*

Awareness surged through her like a current, transforming all her perceptions of him. He was no longer the veterinarian, no longer just a nice person doing her daughter a favor. He was male, large and hulking. He was a *man.* And he was in her kitchen.

Turning her back to him, Angelina frowned as she stirred the sauce, willing it to reach the boiling point so she could escort him out. Out of her kitchen, out of her house and out of her mind.

She wouldn't call what had just happened between them attraction, but it came close enough to make her uneasy. She didn't know anything about him except that he was a veterinarian, he knew how to change tires and he was thoughtful enough to bring a little girl's schoolbooks to her. He probably had a little girl of his own, she decided. Or a little boy. He probably had several children. And a wife. Which meant the sooner she got him out the door and on his merry way home, the better.

"Do you know anything about raccoons?" Lily asked.

"Raccoons?" The vet voiced the question just as the significance of it registered on Angelina.

"You don't have to bother Dr.—" *Why couldn't she ever remember the man's name?* Angelina sucked in a breath. "*Calder* with that, Lily. We're going to the library tomorrow night, remember?"

"But he's a veterinarian," Lily said. "He probably knows lots about raccoons."

"They'll have plenty of books about raccoons at the library," Angelina said firmly.

"Miss Thornton said we can interview someone who knows about animals. She says they're called an authority, and that's the same as looking in a book."

"What's all this about raccoons?" the vet asked. "Is it homework?"

"Uh-huh," Lily replied. "I have to do a report."

"I treat raccoons occasionally."

"Then I can interview you."

"Lily!" Angelina said.

"Miss Thornton said we could interview authorities," Lily persisted.

"Dr. Calder's already taken the time to bring you your books," Angelina reminded her. "He may be in a hurry. He probably has a family waiting for him."

Involuntarily, her gaze met his as she anticipated his response.

"I'm not in a hurry," he said. "And there's no one waiting for me except my dog." His smug male smile told her that he knew she'd been fishing for information.

Serves you right for being so obvious! Angelina chided herself silently, averting her eyes. She hadn't meant to blurt out the comment. She sounded like a desperate woman in a singles bar.

"What do you need to know about raccoons, Lily?" he asked solicitously.

"You really don't have to—" Angelina said.

"I *really* don't mind," he said, winking at her mischievously as she turned just enough to see his face. "It's not every day that raccoon authorities get the respect they deserve."

"I need my binder," Lily said exuberantly, opening her backpack. "I have to take notes!"

At least Lily was excited about her schoolwork, Angelina thought as her daughter and the veterinarian settled at the breakfast nook table for the interview. Lily's teacher was right—Lily was interested in anything that centered on animals.

At last the sauce was ready. Angelina gratefully turned off the burner and poured the sauce over the linguine she'd cooked earlier and the chopped turkey she'd thawed. After mixing the casserole and sliding it into the oven, she glanced at the table where her daughter and Dr. Calder were seated.

Lily was writing with fierce concentration and the vet was idly petting Princess who, after some pestering, had wound up in his lap. Satisfied that she would not be missed, Angelina stole out to her bedroom to brush her hair and put on a fresh coat of lipstick.

Impulsively, she dotted her wrists and the hollow of her neck with the expensive perfume she hoarded for special occasions. After recapping the small bottle, she paused, surprised at what she was doing and contemplating the whimsical impulse that had led her to put on the fragrance. Finally, with a resolute sigh, she placed the bottle back on the vanity and rolled her eyes at her reflection in the mirror. "You need to get out more!" she said aloud.

She was tempted to change her T-shirt. It was a gag gift from her best friend. Angelina never wore it in public, but it was big and comfortable and great to schlepp around the house in. But as embarrassing as it was to be caught in the garish thing, changing it would be too obvious, an admission that she had something to be embarrassed about. She did, however, slip on some flats. She might be stuck with If You're Rich, I'm Available on her chest, but she refused to run around barefoot in front of a man she hardly knew, especially one who'd looked at her the way the man sitting at her kitchen table had.

"Raccoons do something a little unusual," the vet was explaining when Angelina returned to the kitchen. "They wash their food before they eat it."

"Like Mommy washes fruits and vegetables?"

"Well, they don't have sinks like your mother has in her kitchen, but if there's water around, they'll dunk their food in it."

"I hate to interrupt," Angelina said, "but all this talk about raccoons must be making you thirsty. Would you like some milk or juice?"

"Juice!" Lily said.

"You might try 'please' along with that," Angelina coaxed, and Lily complied.

"That's better," Angelina said, turning her attention to Dr. Calder.

"I'll have juice, too," he said, and added, grinning, *"please."*

Angelina nodded and walked to the refrigerator. As she reached inside for the juice, she heard the vet whisper conspiratorially to Lily, "I almost forgot."

Angelina pretended not to hear his comment—or the gasp of suppressed laughter from her daughter which followed. It was so good to see Lily's eyes alight with harmless mischief, her young face relaxed and open instead of pinched with unnatural seriousness.

For the light in her daughter's eyes, more than for the flat tire he'd changed or the schoolbooks he'd delivered or the help he was giving Lily with her report, Angelina owed the veterinarian a debt of gratitude. That indebtedness disturbed her. The good deeds were piling up fast, and she didn't know him well enough to owe him anything beyond a courteous thank-you.

She studied him as surreptitiously as possible as she poured the juice into glasses. As little as she knew about him, she would have been hard-pressed to find a man who seemed less like a stranger.

He was, she decided, more *average* than anything else. His well-broken-in sneakers, his no-designer-label jeans, the T-shirt with the name and dog-and-cat logo of his clinic on his chest made him seem accessible and familiar.

He was tall enough to be taller than most women wearing heels, broad chested enough to project an impression of strength and gregarious enough to have been raised in the house next door. His features were rugged but attractive, his green eyes expressive, his eyelashes lush, his sandy brown hair thick. And his smile, as he acknowledged the juice she set before him on the table, was . . . quite nice. It lingered in Angelina's mind as she turned to set the other glass of juice in front of her daughter.

"You smell good, Mommy," Lily said, yanking Angelina from deep thought.

"I—" Angelina broke off guiltily. She drew in a breath before improvising, "I've been cooking. It must be the Parmesan."

"No," Lily said matter-of-factly. "You don't smell like cheese. You smell like flowers."

"Or musk."

The wry comment followed a beat of deep silence. Angelina looked at his face and found him feigning innocence. But he knew. He knew she'd put on perfume. And he was more certain than she was why she'd done it.

Angelina found that annoying. And embarrassing. What was he doing here, anyway, sitting at her table, holding her daughter's sleeping puppy in his lap?

"What's musk?" Lily asked.

It was one of those moments that made a mother wish she'd opted for birth control. "It's—" She stopped, quickly realizing that her pique was not with her daughter, but with the man who'd insinuated himself into their home and inspired her to put on the perfume in the first place. She smiled at the real antagonist with deceptive sweetness. "Why don't you tell her what musk is?"

He countered her challenge with a lift of his eyebrow and, after a second's pause, he slowly tipped his head. A smile twitched at his mouth. "All right. I'll explain it. I happen to know a little about musk. I *am* a veterinarian."

"I'm sure you're an authority on musk, Dr.—" Damn it! Why couldn't she ever remember his name? She'd been doing so well, sounding so witty—

"Calder," he supplied smugly before turning his attention to Lily. "Musk is a substance produced by the male musk deer, sort of like sweat. It has a very strong scent."

"Does it smell like flowers?" Lily asked.

"No. It . . . actually, it doesn't smell all that great, except to female musk deer."

Lily's face screwed up in confusion. "You think my mommy stinks?"

"No, sweetheart," he assured the child with a chuckle of surprise at the question. "Your mom doesn't stink."

"But you said she smelled like musk," Lily pointed out.

"Perfume manufacturers use musk as a base for some perfumes, but they add a lot of scents to it. Like the flowers you smelled in your mother's perfume. The musk just makes the scent stronger and makes it last longer."

"Mommy can't afford perfume. It's too expensive," Lily said.

Oh, and thank you very much, Angelina thought. *Why don't you take out my checkbook and show him the black ink fading into red?* "I was given a free sample at the mall last weekend," she improvised quickly. "I was checking to see how it works with—"

She stopped abruptly, leaving the sentence hanging, hoping he'd let the subject drop and wishing she'd never put on the perfume in the first place.

He didn't let her off that easily. "With?".

"My body chemistry," she rasped, as though she had a popcorn hull caught in her throat. How had she gotten herself into this conversation, anyway?

"Body chemistry?" His tone was suggestive.

Flustered, Angelina explained, "You're supposed to see how . . . a fragrance . . . interacts when you . . . have it on your skin a while."

"Whatever you're wearing is interacting with your chemistry just fine," he said.

"I have to check on the tetrazzini," Angelina said, hastily retreating to the kitchen. There was no actual need to check on the casserole, but she opened the oven door and peered inside as though without her close supervision the dish might meet with disaster.

Next she foraged through the refrigerator for salad ingredients—anything to appear busy while she regained her equilibrium. It was just so unexpected having a strange man in her house discussing raccoons. And body chemistry.

The sooner he and Lily were finished with the interview, the better.

Snippets of their conversation reached her as she washed the lettuce. "—avid curiosity... very mischievous—"

She turned off the tap and shook the lettuce to remove excess water.

"Wild animal that shouldn't be kept in captivity..."

Surely he would run out of raccoon trivia soon. She washed the cucumber, turned off the tap, trained her ear for signs that they were winding up their discussion.

They were... *giggling*. Technically, Lily was giggling. The vet was chuckling, producing a distinctly male rumble that ricocheted crazily through her nervous system.

Angelina propped her elbows on the counter and her chin on her fists and feigned nonchalance as she spoke to them through the service window. "What's so funny about raccoons?"

"It's not raccoons," Lily said. "Dr. Calder's tummy rumbled."

The vet grinned sheepishly. "It's whatever your mother's cooking in there that smells so good. I got busy today and worked through lunch."

"You could eat with us," Lily said.

"Oh, I couldn't impose," he said, but his objection was halfhearted, as if he wanted to stay but was declining out of good manners.

He was waiting for her to talk him into staying, Angelina realized.

"We're having tetrazzini," Lily persisted. "There's always lots of tetrazzini."

"But . . ." The vet paused hopefully.

Angelina wasn't sure she wanted him to stay for dinner. There was a dangerous intimacy about sitting at the same table and eating from the same casserole dish with a man, especially one who'd been discussing body chemistry. Still, he had been thoughtful enough to bring Lily's books, he'd helped Lily with her report and he'd changed her tire.

"You're welcome to stay," she said. "Lily's right. There's more than enough to go around. It's impossible to make a small batch of tetrazzini."

Although he appeared to want to accept the invitation, he hesitated, as though debating whether or not he should. That surprised Angelina. He didn't seem the type who would ever wrestle with uncertainty, especially after almost inviting himself with that crack about how good the food smelled.

"After all the favors you've done for Lily and me today, the least we can do is feed you a square meal," Angelina said.

His smile came too readily. "If you're sure . . ."

Angelina wasn't sure at all, not with the funny things his smile did to her insides, but she was stuck with him through dessert.

Dessert! What was she going to have for dessert? There wasn't enough time to bake anything. Or make anything. Maybe there was something in the freezer. Yes! There was vanilla ice cream. Plain, but simple. She'd add some chocolate sprinkles, and a couple of vanilla wafers and pretend she was serving mousse.

She finished the salad, put on the green beans and went into the dining room to set the table. Damn! The puzzle she and Lily had been working on for weeks sprawled over the tabletop. She couldn't possibly move it without undoing all their work. They'd have to eat in the breakfast nook.

"Mommy?"

Angelina turned. Lily was standing in the doorway. "Princess woke up from her nap and Dr. Mike says—"

Dr. Mike?

"—she probably needs to go outside now. He said to ask if it's okay."

"When a puppy's gotta go, a puppy's gotta go," the doctor said, walking up behind Lily with the dog still cradled in his arms.

"Then I'd suggest you hurry," Angelina replied.

He followed Lily to the door and said, on his way out, "Don't worry, Mom. We won't be gone long."

The last thing Angelina heard as the door closed behind them was Lily's giggle.

Angelina was setting the table when they returned a few minutes later.

"Princess was a *goo-oo-d* puppy," Lily announced.

"Good for her!" Angelina said.

"Are we using place mats?" Lily asked, making it sound as though she'd never eaten off a place mat in her life.

"Yes," Angelina replied, trying to hide her exasperation. "We're using place mats. And you need to put Princess in her cage, wash your hands and put the silverware on the table, please."

With a shrug of acquiescence, Lily called the dog and led her away, leaving Angelina alone with the veterinarian.

"You shouldn't go to so much trouble on my account," he said.

"I'm not."

"But the place mats—"

"Place mats aren't trouble." Angelina ventured a sly smile. "A tablecloth would be trouble."

Mike wasn't gullible enough to believe her. The place mats *were* trouble. The fact that she'd put on perfume was trouble. The fact that her kid was cute was trouble. Her *smile* was trouble.

All things considered, Mike figured that as far as Mrs.
Winters was concerned, he was hip-deep in trouble and
sinking fast. He was crazy for being here. He'd planned
to hand off the kid's schoolbooks like a relay runner's
baton and make a quick getaway, but here he was, getting ready to sit down to a home-cooked dinner. Home-
cooked by the woman he'd vowed to avoid. Who was
setting the table with place mats she didn't routinely use
and wearing perfume she usually didn't wear.

He watched her fold a napkin and position it just so on
the mat, smoothing it with her fingertips before moving
on to the next place and repeating the process. The aroma
of the casserole baking in the oven floated in from the
kitchen, redolent with spices and cheese.

Lily returned and, after assuring her mother she'd
washed her hands thoroughly, she put out the knives and
forks. Mrs. Winters brought out trivets, centered them
on the table and returned to the kitchen for the casserole.

Trivets. Mike looked at the colorful woven straw circles. What *was* he doing here? He didn't need a Mrs.
Winters complicating his life, and it was obvious that,
perfume aside, Mrs. Winters wasn't thrilled about an
unexpected dinner guest. But he'd practically invited
himself with that comment about how good the food
smelled, and then he'd blithely failed to take advantage
of the opportunities Mrs. Winters had given him to de-
cline the invitation.

A few minutes later, the food was on the table, the
casserole steaming, the bread tucked in a basket, the red

tomatoes nestled in the lettuce like bulbs on a Christmas tree.

Lily said grace, a simple, rhyming verse of prayer softened by her sweet voice.

"The dish is hot," Mrs. Winters said, dipping a spoon into the creamy noodle concoction. "I'll serve your plate."

She smiled warmly at Mike as he gave her his plate, and he felt himself slipping deeper into the mire of potential trouble. Those eyes. That mouth. The way her dark hair curled against her neck.

He should have gone home.

Home? What was he thinking? Home, eating alone? Serving himself institutional-tasting stew taken from a can and using a veterinary supply catalog for a trivet? Watching reruns of insipid sitcoms?

"Dr. Mike!"

He blinked out of his reverie.

Lily, holding the breadbasket, regarded him with an expression of exasperation. "Don't you want bread? It's vampire bread."

"Vampire bread?" he asked curiously.

"The garlic keeps vampires away," Mrs. Winters explained.

"Vampires don't like garlic," Lily said.

"You, uh, have a lot of problems with vampires in this neighborhood?" Mike asked Mrs. Winters, cocking an eyebrow.

"Only the ones Lily saw in a scary movie at her best friend's slumber party," Mrs. Winters replied with an intriguing smile. "They've been fond of garlic bread ever since."

"I see," Mike said, taking a slice. "Say, Lily, you're not testing me, are you, to make sure I'm not a vampire?"

"No," Lily said with a giggle. "We always have vampire bread with tetrazzini."

"I'm not sure I've ever had tetrazzini before," he said.

"It's just a creative way to use leftover turkey after the holidays," Mrs. Winters said.

"Daddy doesn't like turkey sandwiches," Lily said. "That's why Mommy had to learn to make tetrazzini."

Though she tried to hide it, Mrs. Winters's reaction to the mention of her ex-husband was immediate and intense.

Mike pretended not to notice the sudden tension in her features as he sampled a forkful of the pasta and hummed an appreciative, "Mmm. This beats a dry turkey sandwich any day. It's delicious."

"Thank you," Mrs. Winters replied tersely, still noticeably unnerved.

One more reason you should have gone straight home after work! Mike scolded himself.

4

NO MATTER how many times he read the list, the bottom-line analysis didn't change. On a scale of one to six, six being the perfect score, Mrs. Winters scored a miserable one and a half.

They hadn't discussed her job, but Mike assumed, from her response to the idea of having to buy new tires, that she did not have a job that paid well. She had a child, which cost another point. She got half a point for not talking about her ex-husband, although the subject was clearly a sensitive one with her. No points for the car with bald tires, or the house with landscaping that cried out for some heavy-duty pruning.

Her only full point came from the sixth-and-last item on the list: sexy. And that meant trouble, with a capital *T*, as far as Mike was concerned. After dinner last night, he'd helped with the dishes. Then they'd walked the dog together—he, Mrs. Winters and the little girl. And when Mrs. Winters walked him to the door, he'd damned near kissed her good-night.

They'd stood in the entryway, suddenly at a loss for words after she thanked him for bringing the books and changing her tire and he thanked her for dinner. Not quite looking at each other, yet each acutely aware of the other. He, debating whether he should kiss her. She, probably debating whether she should let him if he tried.

The moment had been charged with indecision; it could have gone either way. But Mike had stopped himself just in time, which, in retrospect, was a good thing, considering that he was having a hard enough time trying not to think about her without the memory of a kiss to contend with.

"You're lucky that piece of paper doesn't burst into flame the way you're scowling at it."

Roused from deep contemplation, Mike jarred to attention. "Suzie! Did you say something?"

"Only that you're giving that wall a look that would make a tyrannosaurus rex cower."

"I was just . . . thinking," Mike said.

Suzie cocked her head. "Must be some dark thoughts."

Mike dismissed the observation with a shrug. "Nothing a long-legged blonde couldn't make me forget."

Sniffing her disdain for the idea, Suzie said, "Well, I can't help you. I'm fresh out of long-legged blondes."

"The *world*," Mike said dryly, "is fresh out of long-legged blondes."

"Maybe you should try redheads."

"I did. She's in California with her jerk ex-husband." He paused. "So how was bingo last night?"

"Inez won an electric can opener."

"Again?"

"The fourth this year."

"What does she *do* with them all—or should I ask?"

"She gives them away as wedding presents, of course. Between her kids and grandkids, someone's always getting married."

Someone else, Mike thought morosely.

"Speaking of getting married," Suzie said, "what's going on with Tracy these days?"

"She's going crazy juggling classes and wedding plans. She's trying to keep it simple, but—"

"'Simple wedding' is an oxymoron," Suzie said.

"It is when the mother of the bride gets involved," Mike agreed. "Mother called last night to inform me that the men will be wearing tuxedos."

"Tuxedos? Didn't you just buy a suit for that wedding?"

"Yes, I did. But suddenly all the men have to match— even the older brother who's giving the bride away. I *hate* tuxedos—those dinky little studs, and those cummerbund things, and bow ties—"

He'd sworn the last time he wore one that he wouldn't wear another except to his own wedding.

"It'll only be for a few hours," Suzie said. "After all, your only sister doesn't get married every day."

"Thank God!" Mike said. *His baby sister was beating him to the altar.*

"The secret to tuxedos is to get a woman to put you together," Suzie said.

"I'll manage the pants and shirt on my own and then throw myself on the mercy of the bridesmaids."

"Maybe one of them will be a long-legged blonde."

"Not a chance," Mike said. "I've met both of them. One is engaged to a football player, and the other giggles constantly. Of course, she *is* a blonde."

"That's the attitude," Suzie said, giving his arm a pat. "Keep yourself open to possibilities."

Mike grunted noncommittally. A giggly coed a year younger than his baby sister wasn't his idea of stimulating companionship. His taste ran more toward dark-haired women with kind brown eyes and a beautiful smile—or at least it had for the past eighteen hours. But it was Friday, and the weekend stretched ahead of him, filled with the promise of new women to help him get his mind off a certain dark-haired woman.

"Are you ready for the first patient?" Suzie asked. "It's Fairchild."

"He's not ailing, is he?" Mike asked, concerned. Fairchild was a veterinarian's dream—an immaculately groomed Afghan hound with an excellent disposition and beautiful manners.

Suzie shook her head. "Routine exam. Rabies shot and heartworm preventive."

Mike grinned. "Bring old Fairchild in."

There were worse ways to start off a morning.

Twelve hours later, he was perusing the menu in a trendy Italian eatery. He and his friend Jerry had spent the preceding ninety minutes in the bar nursing a bottle of Chianti while waiting for a table. Jerry had promised that the restaurant would be crowded and noisy, and it lived up to his promise. It was an upscale hangout for thirty-something singles. Like Mike. And Jerry, who had worked past the shock of the breakup of a six-year marriage and was determined to prove he still produced enough testosterone to turn a female head. He seemed to be equally determined that Mike should do the same, leaping into the role of Mike's social planner following the wedding that didn't happen.

There were women at the bar. Mike and Jerry had flirted mildly with a pair of computer technicians in town for a training seminar at AT&T, but the arrival of several more people from the seminar had ended the flirtation before it developed into anything.

Mike was, frankly, relieved when their names were called for a table before they had a chance to strike up a conversation with anyone else. Intellectually, he wanted to play the game, but his heart was no longer in the chase. Perhaps it was a lingering emotional ennui from the broken engagement, but Mike suspected it was more. He'd been on the merry-go-round too long. He was passing the same scenery over and over again. He was just plain tired of the courtship rituals—the speculative glances, the getting-to-know-you questions, the trying-to-impress-you gestures, the wondering where you stood.

"Our special tonight is chicken tetrazzini, which is linguine with a Parmesan cream sauce," the server said.

"That sounds good," Jerry said. "I'll have that."

"And you?" the server said, looking at Mike.

"Spaghetti," Mike said flatly, snapping his menu shut. "With classic tomato sauce and meatballs."

The man nodded and collected the menus. "I'll be right back with your salads and garlic bread."

"To keep the vampires at bay," Mike mumbled.

"Beg your pardon?" Jerry said.

"I said," Mike replied, "that the garlic on the bread will keep vampires at bay."

Jerry rolled his eyes. "Yeah. Sure. Vampires."

Mike was oblivious to his friend's exasperation. His attention was focused several tables away on a woman with hair the color of Mrs. Winters's.

"ARE YOU GOING to take Princess's temperature again?" Lily asked.

"Yep," Mike replied, lifting the puppy's tail. Princess was in for her routine exam.

"And give her a shot?"

"Uh-huh. She has to have the whole series in order to get the protection she needs."

Lily's face pinched in concentration as she watched Mike work. Finally, with a winsome sigh, she said, "I'm glad I'm not a puppy."

"You don't think you'd like going to the vet, huh?"

The child, with her characteristic seriousness, responded with a slow shake of her head.

"Not even a nice vet like me?" Mike cajoled.

"Not if you gave me a shot every time."

Mike chuckled and took a doggie biscuit from a jar on the counter. "How about if I gave you a vitamin cookie?"

"Does it taste good?"

He held the biscuit near the puppy's nose and she quickly snapped it up. "Princess seems to think so."

"I still wouldn't like shots," Lily said cagily.

"Then it's a good thing you're a girl and not a puppy, isn't it?"

"Uh-huh."

Mike read the dog's chart. "You must be feeding Princess well. She's gained three and a half pounds."

"Mommy says she eats like a piglet instead of a puppy," Lily replied.

"Where is your mommy? Isn't she with you today?" He hated himself for asking, hated even more the way his insides tensed as he waited for the little girl's reply.

"She had to go grocery shopping. Princess can't go in the store, so she said for me to take care of Princess and she'd be back in a few minutes. The lady at the desk said it was okay."

"I see," Mike said, wondering why he was annoyed that Mrs. Winters was dodging him when he should have been relieved. After all, he'd spent the last three weeks trying not to think about her.

He finished the examination, administered the dreaded injection and gave Lily a vitamin biscuit to reward the puppy for good behavior.

He tried to resist the urge to follow the child back to the waiting room. He tried—and failed. But a quick glance around the room told him Mrs. Winters was not there. Lily sat down, cradling her puppy in her lap, and became engrossed in the documentary about dogs playing on the VCR. Mike shuffled over to the examining room, where an aging Siamese cat with a nasty kidney infection awaited his professional attention.

After treating the cat, he went to the utility room to wash up before his next patient. *Mike Calder's Minimum Requirements for a Woman* stared at him from the wall as he soaped his hands. Well, good. He needed something to remind him that he was lucky not to have seen Mrs. Winters—Mrs. One-Point-Five-Out-of-a-Possible-Six Winters, who was just the type of woman who'd prompted him to write his manifesto in the first place.

To reinforce the thought, he picked up a pen and wrote, "Winters 1.5." in the margin of the list.

One more patient, and he was finished for the day. Then—

He'd call Jerry, he decided. Jerry was always ready to go schmoozing through noisy nightspots in search of women. Not that they ever found any—at least, not any that Mike was interested in for anything beyond superficial conversation. Jerry wasn't as particular.

He left a message on Jerry's answering machine before seeing his last patients of the day, a mother cat with four kittens in for a routine health screening and worming. Distracted by the antics of the squirmy kittens, he had momentarily forgotten about Mrs. Winters by the time he helped the cat owner carry the menagerie to the reception desk.

She was standing at the desk, chatting with Suzie as they waited for the receipt rolling off the computer printer. Mike smiled involuntarily as he recognized her and, for an instant, Mrs. Winters's face registered surprise mirroring his own. Then she returned his smile, and his hello.

"Lily tells me you were grocery shopping," Mike said.

She nodded self-consciously. "I hope you didn't mind my letting Lily come in alone. The supermarket was right there, and I would have had to take the dog home and come back."

"Lily's welcome here anytime," Mike told her.

The silence that followed was approaching awkwardness, when the printer ground to a halt. Suzie ripped off the receipt and slid it across the counter to Mrs. Winters, who glanced at it briefly before stuffing it into her handbag. She seemed flustered suddenly.

"Your puppy's in great shape," Mike said. "She's extremely healthy."

"She's full of energy."

"Puppies usually are."

"I . . . uh . . ." She flicked her tongue across her lips nervously. "The groceries are in the car. The milk—" She was backing away as she spoke. She was noticeably tense, and Mike wondered if she felt the attraction between them as strongly as he did.

"Lily," she said, looking in her daughter's direction. "Come on. It's time to go."

Mike didn't want her to leave. What he really wanted was to be alone with her.

He should have kissed her, he realized. Consequences be damned, he should have kissed her when he'd had the chance, when they were standing together in her house trying not to look at each other and wondering what it would be like. If he'd kissed her, at least he wouldn't still be wondering.

"Look, Dr. Mike." Lily's voice brought Mike back to reality. "Princess doesn't pull on the leash like she used to."

"Hey!" he said. "You must have been practicing the way I showed you."

"Uh-huh," Lily said. "We go walking every night, and I make the leash short and make her walk right beside me."

"You're doing a good job training her. Now when she gets big, she won't drag you all over the place."

Mrs. Winters had reached the door. She opened it and held it ajar with her hip and shoulder, her impatience evident as she waited for Lily and the dog to pass through.

Lily paused in the doorway. "Bye, Dr. Mike."

"Goodbye, Lily. You take care of that puppy now."

ANGELINA WAS NOT smiling as she got in the car. She pulled out of the parking lot onto the highway with a feeling of immense relief. *You take care of that puppy now!*

It wasn't enough that the man was as sexy as an improper proposition. No! He had to be *nice*, too!

She didn't need this. No. Not at all. She'd felt like a freak ever since her marriage broke up because she wasn't interested in men *that way;* then, when she finally met a man who raised her temperature, he was *nice*.

Nice. Sexy. But not interested.

When he'd stayed for dinner at her house, she'd thought maybe he'd call and ask her out. And in the three weeks since, she'd spent a lot of idle moments contemplating why she wouldn't want to be sixteen again. For a few days she'd been hopeful and expectant. After a week, she'd begun to ponder possible reasons he hadn't called. By the end of two weeks, she had a whole list of reasons why no man in his right mind would *ever* call a thirty-three-year-old single mom who wore shirts that said If You're Rich, I'm Available. Especially after he'd seen how bald her tires were.

Avoiding him had seemed like a judicious course of action and she'd almost succeeded. But then, there she was, writing out another check for five dollars for the "new puppy special" and feeling like the charity case she was, when who should appear but Himself the Veterinarian. And the first thought in her mind was that his eyes were as green as she remembered them.

She'd wanted to slap a fifty-dollar bill on the counter and say that she didn't need new puppy specials, thank you very much. But she didn't have a fifty-dollar bill. Women who'd just bought a full set of tires couldn't afford grandiose gestures like that. On the salary she brought home, she couldn't afford that much pride.

"Dr. Mike gave Princess a cookie," Lily announced.

"That's nice," Angelina said, refusing to succumb to the tears burning the rims of her eyes. *Damn him!* Damn him for being so nice and so...male. For making her feel so . . . female.

She brought the car to a stop at a red light.

"Is Dr. Mike ever going to come see us again?" Lily asked.

Angelina drew in a deep breath and released it. "I don't think so."

"Why not?"

"Well . . ." She looked at her daughter's face, so serious and sincere. "Last time, he came over because he was bringing your backpack to you, remember? He doesn't have a reason to come over again."

"He could come because he likes us," Lily said confidently. "He likes Princess, too."

"I'm sure he likes most of his patients and their owners," Angelina said, "but—"

The car behind her gave a raucous honk, and she snapped to attention. The light was green, and traffic in the lane next to her was already moving steadily. With a gasp of exasperation, she pressed the accelerator.

"But what?" Lily asked.

"What?" Angelina said abstractedly, concentrating on maneuvering the car in the thick commuter traffic.

"You said he likes his patients but. But what?"

"Veterinarians don't usually go to the houses where their patients live," Angelina told her.

"He could be our friend," Lily suggested hopefully.

"Yes," Angelina agreed, her patience waning. "But not all friends visit your house. You have friends that you see at school, and friends that you play with at the park. You can be Dr. . . . *Calder's* friend and see him when you take Princess to the clinic for her checkups."

Lily didn't reply immediately. Angelina relaxed a bit, hoping the subject was dropped for good. For a blissful minute she thought it had been. Then Lily said, "You could invite him to come over."

"I can't do that."

"Why?"

Angelina let out an exasperated sigh. Why indeed? How was she supposed to explain to a seven-year-old that the veterinarian made her pulse race?

"I have to concentrate on driving right now, Lily," she hedged. "Why don't you sing the baby bumblebee song for me?"

Much to her relief, Lily began to sing.

Some things, Angelina thought fatalistically, were even worth enduring the baby bumblebee song for. Getting Lily's mind off Dr. Mike...whatever-his-last-name-was was one of them.

5

THE SHOPPING CENTER where the neighborhood rabies vaccination clinic was set up was in the middle of a three-day, center-wide sidewalk sale. Crowds of weekend shoppers, a popcorn cart outside the supermarket and a pair of roving clowns making balloon animals created a carnival-like atmosphere.

The outdoor clinic was set up in front of a vacant store, sandwiched between a crafts store unloading Halloween masks and other out-of-season holiday items, and an import store offering animal-shaped wicker planters. The clinic consisted of three six-foot tables forming a U-shaped booth. Pet owners lined up with pets of all shapes and sizes, many of which were nervous, unaccustomed to being anywhere but in their own backyards.

The sponsoring association, Common Pet Sense, had arranged for three volunteers to work in the booth with him. Mike introduced himself and found them all energetic and enthusiastic as they thanked him for donating his time to their program.

The line of pet owners with pets to be immunized remained constant all morning. Except for an occasional skirmish between dogs and ill-tempered cats, everything went smoothly. One of the volunteers tended the registration desk and gave out brochures on responsible pet care. A second volunteer, an older gentleman who had a way with animals, distributed the metal tags and put them on collars if asked, while his wife, a registered nurse, assisted Mike with the syringes and vaccine.

Mike was so busy that he could hardly believe it when the woman handling the paperwork commented that the lunch relief team was overdue. Samantha Curry was commuting from location to location with a full staff of volunteers and a veterinarian to give each of the teams a half-hour lunch break.

"There they are now!" said Emma, the nurse, nodding toward a Common Pet Sense van pulling into the parking lot.

Mike's chest tightened a bit in anticipation. He was finally going to meet Samantha Curry. Ms. Curry, with the throaty, purrlike voice. The one who, if she proved as sexy as that voice, would rank a perfect six on his *Minimum Requirements for a Woman* scale.

It wasn't difficult to pick her out of the entourage as it approached. The vet was in a lab coat, the volunteers in CPS T-shirts. Ms. Curry was in beige tailored slacks and a cream-colored silk blouse. Her jaw-length hair, three perfectly blended shades of auburn, was tousled with a seeming nonchalance that comes only from an expensive cut and styling products sold only in salons.

"Samantha looks stunning today," the nurse said under her breath.

"Positively lethal," the other female volunteer said in the same derisive tone.

Samantha Curry was clearly in charge. No one who saw the group walking toward the booth would question her air of authority. And even in the miasmic atmosphere of alcohol wipes, vaccine and nervous canines, she smelled of flowers and sunshine as she extended her hand to him in greeting.

Taking her hand in his, Mike noted the softness of her skin. Her voice was even huskier than it had been over the phone as she thanked him profusely for dedicating his Saturday to Common Pet Sense.

She asked the team if they'd had any problems, if they had plenty of supplies, if they'd had a good turnout, nodding as they gave the responses she wanted to hear.

"The line's backing up," the woman handling the paperwork said sharply. "*Someone* needs to start giving shots."

Ms. Curry responded with an icy smile. "You're absolutely right. Let's change teams so you can go to lunch."

She turned to Mike. "I have the delightful job of accompanying our doctors to lunch—unless you have prior plans?"

She framed the last phrase as a question. "No," Mike said quickly. "No plans at all. I'm all yours, Ms. Curry."

"For thirty minutes," she replied with what sounded like an intentional note of suggestiveness. "Thirty minutes," she repeated, louder, for all to hear. "Please don't be late. The relief team has another stop after this one and we're already off schedule."

They went to a submarine-sandwich shop a few doors down from the clinic. Mike ordered the house special. Ms. Curry ordered cappuccino, but had to settle for de-caffeinated coffee, the taste making her wrinkle her nose with each sip. Her nose was quite perfect, Mike noticed, ignoring the little voice in the back of his head telling him it was *too* perfect—along with the rest of Ms. Samantha Curry.

Ridiculous, he told himself. A woman couldn't be *too* perfect. He was just used to the ones that didn't come anywhere close—women without the smell and look of money, who didn't have the time or resources to work as hard at it as an heiress.

As he ate, she chatted about the clinics at the locations she'd visited. One had been extremely busy, but at the second, the pet owners had come in fits and starts. It was busy one minute, not busy the next. She reiterated the importance of the clinics and the opportunity they presented to educate people on responsible pet ownership. Then, abruptly, she was silent, staring at Mike.

Mike lifted an eyebrow. "Is something wrong?"

Very slowly, keeping her gaze level with his, she smiled. There was a glint in her eyes that was purely predatory. "I just *love* to watch a man eat," she purred. "There's something so . . . *primal* about it."

Mike grinned what he hoped was a sufficiently sensual grin. *And he'd been worried that he might have to do some fancy footwork to get her interested in going out with him.*

He finished his sandwich and put his wadded napkin onto his plastic plate with an air of finality. Ms. Curry responded with a meaningful glance at her watch and a gentle moue that said, "Too bad, but—"

He took the liberty of putting his hand on the small of her back as they walked back to the booth. If he'd overstepped any boundaries, she showed no sign of it. If anything, she moved closer to him. Her leg brushed against his as she moved, and her shoulder lightly touched his chest from time to time.

Definitely interested, Mike thought. He'd wait a couple of days, then give her a call and suggest something a couple of weekends away. He'd check the calendar section of the newspaper and see if there was anything artsy going on.

His mental vision of the two of them dressed to the nines and going into a concert hall was shattered abruptly when he caught a glimpse of a woman disappearing into the discount store they were passing. A woman with dark, shoulder-length hair. A woman about the same height as Mrs. Winters. A woman with the same physical proportions as Mrs. Winters.

Mrs. Winters. He was ninety-nine percent sure. Ninety-nine point nine. He could tell by the way his heart skipped a beat when he saw her. By the way just a glimpse of her was enough to distract him from the woman upon whom he ought to be concentrating his full attention.

Well, he was not so easily distracted! To prove it, he pressed his palm a little more firmly into the curve of Ms.

Curry's back and consciously took note of how good body-warmed silk felt under a man's hand.

The volunteers were approaching from the opposite direction when they reached the booth. Ms. Curry consulted her watch again. "Great. Two minutes early. If we don't hit any traffic, we'll make the last station right on time."

She shook hands with each of the volunteers before they returned to their respective jobs, then focused her full attention on Mike as their hands entwined. The message in her eyes could not be misinterpreted: "I want to know you *much* better."

Mike smiled a promise that he'd see to it that she did.

He watched her lead her band of volunteers through the parking lot, admiring the way she moved. *Wednesday*, he thought. *Definitely Wednesday.*

"Dr. Calder?" It was the nurse. "The line's backing up."

"Bring on the next patient!" Mike said enthusiastically.

The next patient was a mutt of indistinguishable breed. "Hey, buddy, what's your name?" Mike asked.

"It's Charlie," his owner said. He was a boy about ten years old, with freckled cheeks and a flattop haircut.

Mike filled the syringe the nurse handed him and pinched up some skin on the animal's body. The boy's grimace was almost comical as Mike prepared to inject the vaccine.

Just like Lily.

Mike clenched his jaw and gave the dog the shot. He wasn't going to get attached to Lily. He wouldn't let her melt his heart with those big, serious eyes of hers any more than he was going to be drawn in by her mother's . . . *turkey tetrazzini.*

The line tapered off in midafternoon and attendance became sporadic after that. He was chatting with the volunteers during an interval of inactivity, when he caught sight of a familiar figure sifting through the import-store items displayed on the tables next door: Mrs. Turkey Tetrazzini herself.

He decided to ignore her, unless she spied him and spoke to him first. But despite his resolve, he continued to watch her compare price tags on wicker planters of various sizes, until an elderly gentlemen brought his Pomeranian to the booth.

The dog was old but healthy and alert. Her coat was shiny and thick and it was obvious that she was brushed regularly.

"Who have we here?" Mike inquired genially, stroking the peppy little dog.

"What?" the old gentleman bellowed, cupping his ear with his hand. "Speak up!"

"I said—" Mike raised his voice to accommodate the man's near deafness "—she's a fine little dog. What's her name?"

"Fiji," shouted the man. "Like the island . . . My wife's dog . . . She's been dead two years."

"That's too bad," Mike said, preparing the syringe.

"Speak up! I can't hear you!"

Mike looked the man squarely in the face and said loudly, "I'm sorry about your wife."

"My wife?" the man responded at rock-concert volume. "My wife's not here. She died two years ago."

"I'm sorry," Mike shouted back, aware that almost everyone in the county was listening to the exchange.

A quick cut of his eyes toward the import store confirmed that the one particular *everyone* he was primarily concerned with, the *everyone* he was ignoring unless fate forced him to do otherwise, was, indeed, listening. Catching him looking at her, she grinned and lifted one shoulder in a sympathetic shrug.

Mike returned to the job at hand and vaccinated Fiji. Fiji's owner scooped the dog into his arms, accepted the collar tag and screamed a thank-you.

"Poor man," said the woman tending the paperwork.

"Bad batteries," the nurse said. "He probably lives alone and doesn't realize they're so weak." She left the booth and ran to catch up with him, tapping him on the shoulder. She gestured to her ear. "Sir, you need new batteries."

"What's that you say?" he roared.

"Fresh batteries," she shouted.

Finally, comprehension dawned. "Have I been talking too loud?" he asked, looking abashed.

She nodded. "We'll watch your dog while you go get them."

"You'll watch Fiji?"

Again she nodded.

"Nurse mode," Emma's husband observed fondly as she took the Pomeranian into her arms.

She returned to the booth and everyone fussed over the little dog, who didn't appear to hold a grudge over having been poked by a needle earlier.

Mrs. Winters had moved on to a table on the far side of the import shop door and was rummaging through a potpourri of small novelty items in a bargain basket.

If he didn't do something to stop her, she was going to leave. All notion of ignoring her evaporated.

"You want to hold Fiji, Dr. Calder?" asked the nurse.

"Uh . . . yes . . . sure. In fact . . . there's someone I'd like to show her to." He'd learned during his teen years that nothing was more irresistible to a female than something cute and fuzzy and little. "I'll be within sight, right over there. If we get any animals to vaccinate, give me a holler."

Nestling the dog in the crook of his arm, he strolled over to Mrs. Winters and waited for her to notice him. Smiling, she put down the napkin ring she'd been pricing. "Who's your friend?" she asked.

"This is Fiji. We're dog-sitting while his daddy shops for batteries for his hearing aid."

She raised her hand to pat the dog's head, but hesitated. "Is she friendly?"

"I think she'd tolerate a little attention."

Fiji got more than a little attention as Mrs. Winters stroked and kneaded the dog's head with her fingertips. Mike could have tolerated a little of the same. He could have endured a lot of it, as a matter of fact.

"You . . . uh, you're giving rabies shots today?"

"My civic duty," he said. "How about you? Are you keeping the economy healthy by supporting the local merchants?"

She sighed dismally and lowered her eyes. "I seem to be supporting some of them a lot more than I'd like to lately."

"Major purchase?" he asked curiously.

"Tires last month." Her gaze lifted to his. "You know all about that. And this week my washer decided to go on the blink."

"You're shopping for a washing machine?"

"*Was* shopping for one. I bought one. There was a sale on at Fred's Furniture and Appliances." She managed to make a frown sexy. "You'd think there would be some joy in spending so much money, instead of—"

Mike couldn't remember when he'd wanted to kiss a woman so badly. He could almost taste the need, it was so intense. But if Mrs. Winters was suffering the same desperate longing, she showed no sign of it.

"The worst part," she said, "is that by the time I get it installed on Thursday, I'll be a week behind in the laundry."

"Thursday? Why wait until Thursday?" Mike asked.

"That's the day the store delivers to my zip code," Mrs. Winters said, frowning again.

"You're having the machine delivered? I thought they charged an arm and a leg for that."

"An arm at least," she agreed. "And I'll probably wind up taking half a day off from work to let the deliveryman in, but I have to have a washing machine, and even if I had a truck, I couldn't get the washer into the house by myself."

Don't say it! he told himself. *Don't offer. You're falling into the same old trap. Her problems are no concern of yours. She bought a washing machine and she's having it delivered. Leave it at that.*

"I have my van here," he said. "If you don't mind waiting until I'm finished at the booth, I could get your washer into your house for you."

"You can't—" She gasped. Color rose in her cheeks. "I couldn't . . . you're always—" She stopped and started anew, stronger. "They're going to deliver it Thursday."

"I don't mind," he said. And he didn't—didn't mind hauling the washing machine, that is. What he minded was getting involved with someone who needed to avoid the delivery charges. "Really. It wouldn't even take half an hour for me to drop it off and hook it up."

She was frowning that sexy frown again.

"You don't want to have to wait until Thursday to do laundry and miss a day of work," he cajoled.

He could see her concentration in the small lines that appeared in her forehead as she considered the situation. She was thinking hard, weighing the pros and cons. "I don't even know if the store has one in stock. They're probably delivering out of a warehouse," she said.

"We won't be closing for another two hours. Why don't you check with the salesman? If they have one available, you can come by the table and tell me."

Intent on watching her face, he was surprised by a tap on the shoulder. "Dr. Calder?"

It was one of the volunteers. "Sorry to interrupt, but you've got some patients waiting."

"I'm on my way." Pausing for one parting glimpse of Mrs. Winters, he told her, "Check it out and let me know."

She nodded, but as he returned to the booth and gave Fiji back to her owner, he would have been willing to bet that Mrs. Winters wouldn't venture within a hundred yards of him if she could avoid it.

Good! He was glad. He really was. Just as he was glad that a woman had brought in her seven cats for vaccinations so that he would have something to think about besides Mrs. Winters and her washing machine.

Seven cats in a strange environment about to be stuck with a needle by a total stranger could make a man forget just about anything.

ANGELINA DIDN'T HAVE cats to distract her. Fleeing the scene of her encounter with the veterinarian, she decided to indulge in a soft pretzel and a soda at the snack bar near the appliance store where she'd bought the washing machine. Since it was something she and Lily usually did when they were at this shopping center, the pretzel break only made her lonesome for Lily, who was spending the weekend with her father. Her father, his new wife, his new wife's kids and his newborn son, to be exact. Lily had dreaded going, and tomorrow she'd come

home more confused than ever about what her role was
in her father's life.

Well done, Thomas, Angelina thought with a scowl.
*You couldn't have done a better job of creating mayhem
in your daughter's life if you'd sat down and plotted it.
Wasn't it enough to make a mockery of our marriage and
all the plans we'd made together?*

She was *not* going to think about Thomas! There was
nothing to be gained from stewing over things she
couldn't change. She'd stew over something more immediate. Like the way her body seemed to turn into a
mass of exposed nerve endings every time she got near
the good Dr. Calder. Or why his green eyes got to her.
Or why she kept noticing his hands. She didn't go around
noticing men's hands. But his were so . . . nice. Strong.
Gentle. Competent.

Listen to yourself! she chided. Gad, she was obsessing
over him like a teenager.

She pondered the phenomenon while slowly devour-
ing her pretzel. Maybe she *was* going through a second
adolescence. Maybe, because her relationship with
Thomas had died, she had to start all over with the man-
woman thing. For almost two years she'd been pretty
much oblivious to men. Then she'd begun to feel the
physical deprivation of not having a man in her life.

At first, it was just the closeness, the warmth of cuddling on a cool night, the security of strong arms around
her. Then came the tension. The unappeased yearning.
The tossing and turning at night, remembering, feeling
the emptiness beside her, the emptiness inside her.

Still, while she was thinking about a man, she hadn't been interested in any man. Her friends had told her she should be dating. She'd allowed them to arrange a blind date or two. She'd enjoyed the company, the adult conversation, the sound of an adult male voice. But she hadn't felt the magic, the unpredictable chemical attraction, the sexual zing.

Until the veterinarian had come into her house, sounding like a man, smelling like a man and looking at her the way a man looks at a woman he's thinking of in a sexual way—making her feel female and desirable. Making her look at him in a sexual way. Reminding her, simply by being there and being virile, how long it had been since she'd been with a man.

He'd almost kissed her. She was sure he'd been considering it. And then—nothing. No call. No further contact at all, unless she counted the postcard reminding that it was time for Princess to have the next in her series of shots.

Angelina wasn't inclined to count the postcard. So, judiciously, she'd avoided seeing him. Or tried to. But she'd seen him, anyway, and it had been the same thing all over: the strong awareness of him as a man, the chemical attraction, the tension.

The hope, the waiting, the disappointment, she added humorlessly. If there was anything she didn't need complicating her life, it was a man who made her feel the way Dr. Calder made her feel—especially when he remained oblivious to his effect on her. She was nothing but a . . . a . . . *charity case* to him.

The tire. Lily's books. The new puppy special for poverty-stricken single mothers with bald tires. The washing machine—

Imagine him offering to haul her washing machine home and install it to save her the delivery fee!

Bracing her elbow on the table, she rested her chin on her fist. He was just . . . so . . . *nice!* As she saw it, it was his most dangerous trait. If he weren't truly nice, she could dislike him, and if she disliked him, she might not be so attracted to him. Of course, he'd still have those green eyes. And those hands—

She exhaled a languid sigh. Too bad she couldn't take him up on the offer about the washing machine. She couldn't afford the washer, much less the thirty dollars tacked on for delivery. If not for her raging hormones, she could save money, and he'd have the satisfaction of having done another good deed.

Raging hormones? What was she thinking? She was Angelina Winters. She didn't *have* raging hormones! She might be attracted to the man, but she was a grown woman, not a naive teenager.

The more she thought about it, the sillier the whole thing seemed. It wasn't as if she was a hapless victim of her biological urges. She was a grown woman with a great deal of self-discipline; otherwise, she'd never have been able to hold everything together for Lily and herself. Surely, if she could handle parenthood single-handedly, she could handle a few minutes alone with a nice man who'd offered to do her a favor.

It wasn't as though the attraction was two-sided. He hadn't given her the first indication that he was interested in anything other than her washing machine.

Except for the way he looked at her.

But all men looked, didn't they? What was that old expression? Married, not dead—it doesn't hurt to look. Only he wasn't married, which meant he had an unlimited right to look.

She'd just have to handle the situation better. Saving thirty dollars and not having to spend several hours in a Laundromat on Sunday afternoon were worth the inconvenience of a little ogling.

Her mind was made up. If the washing machine was in stock and could be picked up today, she would take Dr. Calder up on his offer. She'd just put a lid on her lust and take a cold shower after he left.

The machine was in stock. Angelina had the salesman cancel the delivery request and rewrite the sales ticket without the extra charge.

By the time all the arrangements were made and she returned to the vaccination station, it was almost four o'clock. She stood off to the side, waiting for a lull in the line of pet owners who'd waited until the last minute to bring their pets, but the line remained three deep for the ten minutes she stood there watching the vet work.

She'd never thought about veterinarians having a bedside manner, but whatever it was called for those treating animals instead of human beings, Dr. Calder was charming to his patients. He petted each animal, gave it a quick look-over, spoke to the owners and wielded the syringe with competence and authority.

He was, she decided, probably a very good veterinarian. And a very caring human being.

He spied her and grinned widely. Tilting his head toward the back of the booth, he said, "Come on in."

Angelina hesitated, until he said, "We could use some help."

She walked to the far end of the side table and tentatively entered the work area, glad to help, but wondering what they wanted her to do.

"Thank goodness!" said the woman seated at the table where the pet owners were filling out information cards about their pets. She got up and whispered in Angelina's ear. "I have to find a little girls' room." She winked and said in a normal voice, "Just make sure all the blanks are filled in, and if you have any problems, ask Emma. She's the one unpacking the syringes."

She was off at a fast clip, and Angelina sat down and began handing out forms and reviewing them. The regular volunteer returned after a few minutes. "How's it going?"

"Fine," Angelina reported.

"If you can stay a few minutes more, I'll help Emma out with the syringes and vaccine."

"Sure," Angelina said. "I'd be happy to stay."

The line held steady until five o'clock. Finally the volunteer who'd relieved Angelina gave out cards to the five people left in line and said to the last person, "You're our last customer. After you, our clinic is officially closed."

The woman stood there a few minutes, looking official, shooing away last-minute stragglers, while the vet quickly finished the vaccinations.

"That's all, folks!" the nurse said as the last patient, a curly-tailed chow, strutted off at the end of a leash.

Within seconds, the volunteers were busy stacking, straightening and packing. Somewhat overwhelmed by all the activity and feeling superfluous, Angelina moved out of the center of activity. She was asking herself what she was doing there when, suddenly, the vet was standing in front of her. "Thanks for filling in."

"I'm glad I could help," Angelina said.

"What did you find out about the washer?"

"They have one. It'll be waiting at the pickup area behind the store."

"Then let's go get it," he said.

Angelina was sure that he didn't mean anything when he stretched his arm across her back and rested his hand on her waist as they left the booth. It was an automatic reflex to him. He'd have done the same thing if he'd been walking with his grandmother, or his sister.

But the gentle pressure of his hand on her waist certainly didn't make her feel sisterly toward the man attached to the arm stretched across her back. It made her feel like a woman who'd been too long without a man's touch, a woman hungry for physical intimacy. How easy it would be to drift closer to the male warmth of his body, to melt bonelessly into that heat and—

She couldn't prevent what she was feeling, but Angelina refused to dwell on it. Thinking about it would only make the situation worse.

"My car's parked at the other end of the shopping center," she said, quickening her stride so that she walked right away from his loose grasp. "I'll meet you at the pickup window."

"My van's at the end of this row," he said. "Let's pick up the washer, then I'll drop you off at your car on our way to your house."

Trapped by the logic in the suggestion, Angelina accompanied him to the van and tried to ignore how solid his chest felt against her thigh as he helped her up into the high passenger seat.

"Are you sure you have room for a washing machine in here?" she asked, eyeing the back of the van dubiously.

"The back seats are removable," he said. "I'll just stack them against the front seat and the washer will fit just fine."

"That sounds like a lot of trouble," Angelina said as he started the van's engine.

"It's not," he assured her, shifting into reverse.

Angelina peered out the side window as he skillfully maneuvered the van through the crowded parking lot.

"Where's Lily?" he asked after a spell of silence.

"With her father," Angelina replied, trying to keep the rancor out of her voice.

Apparently she was less successful than she'd hoped. "That bad?" he asked.

Angelina paused before answering. "He doesn't intentionally hurt her. He just . . . does."

"Not physically?"

"Certainly not! Do you think I'd let her go with him if I even suspected—"

"Of course not," he said repentantly, with a sigh of frustration. "It was a dumb thing to say."

"There's the pickup dock," Angelina said. *Thank goodness.*

Ten minutes later the machine was loaded in the van and two minutes after that, Angelina was unlocking her own car. She settled into the driver's seat and closed the door with no small measure of relief, glad to be alone, and gladder still that she hadn't had to spend another second closed up with Dr. Calder. He was too male, and she was much too aware of it for her to feel comfortable sitting four inches away from him in a confined space.

She started the engine, fastened her seat belt and took a steadying breath. All she had to do was drive home, get the washing machine into the house, get the veterinarian out of the house and she'd be fine. She could do laundry and watch television and make popcorn for dinner.

Just another fun-filled Saturday night!

They were stopped at a red light less than halfway home when he tapped his horn. Concerned, she twisted so she could see him. He was gesturing for her to pull over, pointing to the entrance of a small shopping center anchored by a supermarket. Assuming there was a problem with the washing machine, she nodded and, when the light turned green, she turned into the parking lot.

He followed, pulled in next to her and hopped out of the van. She rolled down her window. "What's the problem?"

"Do you like fajitas?"

"Fajitas?"

"I'm starving. We just passed Casa Lupe, and I suddenly got a yen for their fajitas. Let's go eat."

"I don't—"

"You don't have plans for dinner, do you?"

"No, but—I—"

"Don't like Mexican food?"

"I like Mexican food just fine, but—"

"Oh, come on. Give a guy a break. If you don't go with me, I'll have to go later by myself."

Angelina frowned, saying nothing.

"Aren't you just a little bit hungry?" he cajoled as if he were a kid begging to stay up late. "Casa Lupe has this 'Fajitas for Two' special where you get all kinds of extras. You'd be doing me a favor."

6

"TOLD YOU there were great extras with the special," Mike said, looking at Angelina across their dishes of fried ice cream—huge, cherry-topped balls of crunch-encrusted ice cream centered on cinnamon-sugared tortillas, drizzled with caramel topping and surrounded by rosettes of piped whipped cream.

"I hope you never decide to talk me into something illegal," she said, picking up her spoon. "I'd probably wind up in jail."

Mike could think of only one thing he'd like to talk Angelina into, and since she was past the age of consent, it wasn't illegal. It was just unwise. He had the washing machine in his van to prove it.

But it was difficult to remember how low Angelina Winters scored on his *Minimum Requirements* scale when she was sitting across the table from him eating fried ice cream. Unconsciously licking caramel from her top lip. *Breathing*—

Angelina. Angelina *Martinez* Winters, he'd learned early in their conversation. The name suited her. She was an angel, all right, all sweetness and goodness, with a flash of Latin fire.

It was almost enough to make him question the relevancy of the whole *Minimum Requirements* thing—until he remembered the washing machine in his van. And the soulful-eyed little girl visiting her father. God only knew what the whole story was there. Angelina tensed up worse than a cat being challenged by a dog every time the subject came up.

"Where did you say you worked?" he asked, deliberately shifting from the brain just below his belt buckle to the one in his head.

"Morgan Printing."

"Printing?" he said. *Printing?* "That sounds interesting."

"Sometimes it is. Sometimes it's not."

"What do you . . . do you run presses?"

"Only in a pinch," she said, mocking his forced interest with a knowing smile. "Technically, I'm a graphic designer."

"That sounds important."

She laughed softly. "It's not. Most of the time it's straight typing. But every once in a while, I get to design something for a customer."

"Like what?"

"Business cards. Invitations. Fliers. Menus. Announcements."

"What kind of announcements?"

"Anything anyone wants to announce. Sales. Grand openings. We're a small printer, so most of our customers are small business owners or individuals. Some of the things we do are just plain goofy."

She sank her spoon into the ice cream. "One couple had adoption notices made up when they adopted a puppy from the animal shelter."

She raised the spoon to her mouth and savored the taste of the ice cream before swallowing it. Mike did the same with his own dessert before asking, "So how does one become a graphic designer?"

"I was majoring in art before—" Her eyes betrayed an old hurt. "I dropped out of college when my ex-husband and I got married. I was going to help him finish getting his degree, then go back and get mine. But—" She sighed softly. "It's the same old story. He graduated and I had a baby. I was planning on going back when Lily started school, but . . . I went to work instead."

"You haven't given up, have you?"

Mike could tell by the expression in her eyes that he'd hit a nerve. "College is not at the top of my list of priorities at the moment," she told him evenly.

"I didn't mean that it should be," Mike said. "It just sounded . . . important to you."

"Maybe someday," she said. "Right now I'm building a portfolio, and in a year or two I hope to get my own equipment and work free-lance out of the house."

"Become an independent businesswoman?"

"I just want to be around in the afternoons when Lily decides she's too old for after-school day care."

The server approached the table, asked if there was anything else they needed and left the check.

"I should get that," she said, oozing guilt as he picked it up.

"Don't be ridiculous. I owe you a meal."

"But . . . the washing machine—"

"Are you trying to bruise my male pride?"

The appalled expression on her face was comical. "No!"

"Well, call me old-fashioned, but when I invite a woman to dinner, I pick up the tab."

IF LITTLE PUFFS of lint under a bed were dust bunnies, the area beneath Angelina's old washing machine was inhabited by a muck monster. Anchored in the sticky mire were a penny, a plastic finger puppet, a shirt button, an open safety pin, a lollipop stick and, as the crowning touch, a zebra-striped organza baby-doll pajama top, which had disappeared shortly after Angelina's fourth wedding anniversary.

"This may well be the most embarrassing moment of my life," Angelina said.

Mike shrugged. "Looks like what I found under my couch the last time I vacuumed."

Angelina bent to grab the ridiculously skimpy garment, hoping to hurl it into the basket of dirty laundry waiting its turn for the new machine, but the sheer top did not come willingly. It yielded with a wretched ripping sound. Angelina looked from it to Mike's face and asked with a raised eyebrow, "Oh, really?"

Mike grinned sheepishly. "Wishful thinking."

"This space will have to be mopped before we bring in the new machine," Angelina said brusquely, her face still pink with embarrassment.

Mike shrugged. "It'll take me a while to get the new one out of the box, anyway."

Angelina found a mop and filled a plastic bucket with water, then attacked the offensive spot on the floor with the force and determination of a sexually deprived woman who has a sexy man in her garage.

An *old-fashioned* sexy man, she reminded herself. Not that his buying dinner was any problem to her. In fact, she'd been damned relieved that he'd paid for the meal. On her budget, she didn't care one whit about striking a blow for a woman's equal right to pay a restaurant tab.

But old-fashioned men liked taking charge of women, taking care of them, pampering them.

Angelina had fallen into that trap once. She'd allowed a man to take charge. Take care of her. Pamper her. *Incapacitate her. Diminish her. Stifle her.* No, thank you. Not again. She wasn't going to wake up one morning on her own, on the edge of destitution, ill-prepared to support herself and her child. She was her own woman now, doing the best she could do. She and Lily had muddled through so far, and they'd continue to manage. She might eventually fall in love, but she was not going to be dependent on any man ever again—especially a man who took pride in being old-fashioned.

She thrust the mop into the water, then scrubbed the spot with unnecessary vigor. Now if she could just figure out what to do about the way her hormones raged every time Mike Calder got within twenty feet of her!

He was in the garage, still pulling packing materials from the washer, when she carried the bucket out to empty it. "Lily and her friends may want to make a playhouse out of the box," he said.

"They'll have a ball with it," Angelina agreed. "Thanks for saving it."

Why did he have to be so thoughtful? Angelina wondered. If he weren't so nice, maybe her heart wouldn't race when he smiled at her. Maybe rooms wouldn't suddenly seem too small when he walked into them. Maybe her temperature wouldn't rise when he touched her.

"She's almost ready to go," he said.

Silence followed. Angelina watched Mike work, observing his concentration, admiring his grace of motion, reacting to his strength with awe. His hands moved deliberately, confidently, efficiently. She imagined them on her flesh, stroking, caressing, stirring up magic. She tasted desire on her tongue, wondering what it would be like if he kissed her.

It was going to be a long half hour before she had him out of her house.

"Do you always travel with a dolly?" she asked as he nosed the platform of the device under the machine.

"Somebody's always moving something," he replied with an affable grin. "It comes in handy."

He maneuvered the dolly with commanding skill, getting the heavy appliance into the house without its slipping or tilting.

"You've done this before," Angelina said.

"I worked for a moving company one summer. This is a piece of cake. You should try getting a piano up a flight of stairs."

"Not in this lifetime," Angelina said.

He positioned the machine about a foot away from the wall and picked up one of the hoses connected to the back. "Now we hook these babies up, plug it in and, presto, you're in business."

Angelina felt claustrophobic suddenly. He was just too male, and she was too aware of it. His firm buttocks strained against his jeans as he bent across the washer to reach the faucets. Golden hair dusted his sturdy arms. Well-honed muscles rippled beneath the knit of his shirt as he worked. His forehead furrowed as he screwed the connectors onto the lip of the faucet.

"Think you could rustle up a flashlight?" he asked.

"Sure," she said, relieved to have an excuse to leave the room.

The flashlight was in the bedside-table drawer in her bedroom. She seized the opportunity to freshen up, splash cold water on her face and generally collect her wits before returning to the laundry room.

"Here you go," she said, offering him the flashlight.

"You're going to have to hold it for me," he said. "I'm going to be practically standing on my head to reach the damn plug."

"Why?"

"Because the cord is short and the hoses are shorter. You don't plug it in before you get the water hoses connected and some idiot electrician thought it was cute to put the plug almost on the floor."

"Couldn't you move the dryer over and go in from the side?"

"Not unless you want to disconnect the vent hose. I wouldn't recommend that. Old hoses tend to be brittle, so unless you want to make a run to a hardware store to replace it—"

Angelina couldn't help it. She giggled.

"What?" he said, giving her a perplexed look.

She could hardly tell him that she was captivated by his masculine approach to the situation, that she found his impatience utterly male, that his churlishness endeared him to her because it was the first hint of imperfection he'd ever allowed her to glimpse. "It just struck me as funny that plugging it in is the most challenging part."

Mike's mouth hardened. His forehead creased and he shook his head ever so slightly, as if to say, "Women!"

Angelina's breath caught at the poignant familiarity of his expression. How could she know him so well when she'd spent so little time with him?

He hitched his backside onto the washer. Then, twisting, stretching and groaning a bit, he reached behind the appliance to position the plug. "Light!" he ordered.

Angelina suspended the flashlight over the rim of the washer, pointing downward.

"To the right," he instructed.

She bent her wrist slightly.

"More," he said.

She was forced to move, bodily, in his direction. Any closer and she'd be *touching* him, her waist against his thigh, and—

"Another inch," he told her.

Gritting her teeth, Angelina pressed closer. Though she expected the reaction, it was nevertheless electric as her side pressed into Mike's. She didn't need wall outlets to feed the surge of pure sexual energy that coursed through her. It was a wonder the washing machine wasn't running through sheer osmosis.

"Good," he said, his voice revealing the physical strain of the contorted position he was in. "Now—"

Without warning, the washing machine sprang to life. *It would be the spin cycle,* Angelina thought, flailing her arm across his back to try to reach the control knob. Since Mike was trying to do the same thing, she managed only to clip his ear with the flashlight and get her arm tangled with his. Her right breast became wedged against his shoulder, and her face was practically buried in his neck, where she received a full helping of his aftershave with each breath.

One of them, she was never sure which, succeeded in getting the knob pushed. Angelina eased away from him, but his fingers wrapped around her wrist, preventing a total retreat. He rolled until they were face-to-face and grinned like the very devil. "I guess what they say about washing machines is all true."

"What they say?" Angelina asked, her voice sounding thin and airy.

"About all the erotic possibilities," he said. His voice was anything but thin and airy. It was as heavy as rich liqueur and dripping with sensual suggestion. He was on his feet now, and standing close enough for the heat of his body to seep into hers. A smug, knowing smile formed on his lips and lust glinted in his eyes as his hands slid up her arms.

Angelina could have pulled away. She should have. She wanted to—or thought she did. But she didn't move. She waited. Waited while the inevitability of the kiss thrummed through her; waited, anticipating, before his mouth actually brushed hers; waited for the rush of sensation that first contact would bring. Needing it. Fearing it. Anxious for it. Dreading it . . .

He cradled her face with his palms, and his gaze locked with hers. There were no questions in the green depths of his eyes, no answers in the bottomless brown of hers. There was only the mutual acknowledgment of the force drawing them together, the mutual acceptance that they were fated to kiss.

He took his time, lowering his mouth to hers slowly and leisurely testing the texture of her lips against his own, but the kiss was no less stimulating for its lack of urgency. The gentle pressure of his mouth on hers became the focus of Angelina's conscious awareness. There was glory in that mating of pliant flesh to pliant flesh. Passion. Promise. Heat.

It had been so long since she'd been kissed this way, since a man had held her with tenderness and made her feel desirable. She abandoned herself to the sheer pleasure of it, sliding her arms around his waist. He was so . . . male, solid and warm and strong.

He lifted his head slightly, breaking the kiss by a fraction of an inch, and she marked the loss with a small moan of regret.

"And I was afraid it was one-sided," he said, his voice husky with arousal. Even if she'd wanted to offer a token denial, she wouldn't have had time before his mouth covered hers again, more insistent than before.

Starting where the first had left off, this kiss was deeper, more impassioned, more intense. It moved beyond the simple touch of mouth to mouth to become totally involving.

Angelina's scalp tingled. Her toes curled. And at all points in between she burned with pleasure and sexual hunger and a need that was both physical and emotional.

His technique was flawless, his hands clever. Angelina reveled in the richness of sensation as those healer's hands generated magic with each artful caress. Angelina sank ever more deeply under the spell of his magic until, suddenly, his hands splayed over her bottom, pressing her body tightly against his. His hardness and heat telegraphed his arousal. The intimacy was too abrupt, too intense. Shocking.

With a cry, Angelina tore away from him. Stunned, struggling for composure, they stared at each other. His eyes were glazed, his cheeks flushed. Angelina knew she must look equally as disheveled and disoriented.

"I—" She broke off, wishing her mind weren't so fogged by the kiss.

"Me, too," he said, moving to pull her back into his arms.

To start up where they'd just left off, Angelina realized. "No!" she said.

Taking a step back, she encountered the washing machine and realized she had no avenue of escape if he chose to trap her there.

"What—" He shook his head in disbelief. "Are you *afraid* of me?"

"No!" she snapped. She was afraid that if she let him start kissing her again, they'd end up naked on the laundry room floor, but she wasn't going to share that news with him.

"Then—"

Angelina drew in a breath, wishing her mind were clearer so she could be more articulate.

Wishing the cartilage in her knees hadn't turned to jelly.

"Dr.—"

"Mike," he said through clenched teeth.

"*Mike.* Look, I appreciate your bringing the washing machine to the house and installing it, but I planned on baking you some cookies or something, not—"

His entire face was a scowl. "You don't think . . ." His voice trailed off into an anguished sigh of frustration.

She didn't, actually. But it was a convenient diversion from the real issue, which was that she was so attracted to him, she was afraid of embarrassing herself. She poised her mouth to speak, hoping that by some miracle, whatever came out would sound remotely intelligent.

But Mike spoke first. And what he said was not just intelligent. It was righteously indignant. "I don't have to move appliances to get a woman to go to bed with me.

And for your information, connecting hoses is not my idea of foreplay."

"Your idea of foreplay is the spin cycle!" Not even *remotely* intelligent, she thought with a sinking sensation in her guts.

"Not until five minutes ago, Mrs. Winters," he said.

She deserved his scorn, she thought. And the look he was giving her: one of those lecherous, frankly sensual looks a man gives a woman in a bar when she's wearing a dress that's too low, too tight and too short. What did she expect when she'd kissed him as though...as though she hadn't been kissed in . . . almost two years.

Stalemate. Silence. *Miserable* silence. Angelina couldn't stand it. "I just think we ought to—" She sniffed indignantly. "I don't even know you!"

"I thought we were getting better acquainted. You *are* the woman I had in my arms, aren't you? The one who—"

"Yes!" she said, her cheeks flaming. "But it's still—"

If looks could kill, she would have been a dead woman under the wrath of his frown. "Relax, Angel. All you have to say is no. I'm not into date rape any more than I'm into seduction on top of major appliances."

Angelina hugged herself and exhaled heavily. She, too, could frown. "This isn't even a date."

And it was about time she remembered it! Remembered the way she'd thought he might call. The way she'd stared at the phone in odd moments, willing it to ring. The disappointment when it didn't. The discouraging thought that if he'd been interested in her, it would have.

"Are you sure about that?" he asked, his usual good humor resurfacing. "It certainly *felt* like a date. I mean, we were rolling fajitas together from the same platter."

"Only because there was a special," Angelina replied.

He chuckled. "Right."

A strained silence ensued. Finally, Angelina broke it. "It might be better if you left."

"Can't," he said.

"Can't? What's that supposed to mean?"

"The machine isn't leveled yet." He grinned. "I couldn't possibly leave a nice woman like you unleveled."

"I don't even know what you're talking about."

"There are some adjustment screws on each corner—"

Her blush must have been obvious because he stopped midsentence and grinned again. Lasciviously.

"Don't say another word!" she snapped.

"Hey. Look. It's important. It really is. If you don't level the machine, it'll vibrate—"

Angelina muttered a word she seldom used and would never, ever have let Lily hear her say. "Then do whatever you have to do and—"

"Get the hell out of here?" he finished for her.

Angelina sighed dismally. "I don't mean to seem ungrateful—" *But I'm so attracted to you that I can't think straight when you're around, and you didn't . . . call.*

"Didn't you level your old machine when you first installed it?"

"I wasn't paying attention, I guess." Just as she'd never paid attention to how to put a fresh spool of line in the weed chopper or how to change the batteries in the smoke detectors or how to fix a leaky faucet.

He tweaked the tip of her nose with his finger. "Trust me, Angel. If you don't level it, your machine will dance around and make funny noises."

"Level it, then. And show me what you're doing."

Kneeling next to the left side, he pointed to the metal disk that she would have called, simply, a foot. "See this? Twist it one way and it gets longer, twist it the other way and it gets shorter. You want to adjust these until—is something wrong?"

He'd caught her staring. Smiling, Angelina shook her head. "You're very patient to explain."

Would Thomas have explained things to her if she'd asked? She honestly didn't know; she'd never thought to ask. She'd never thought that her marriage would end and she'd have to take care of the things she'd always left up to him. Now, in reflection, she realized that she'd never done much thinking at all.

Maybe that's why Thomas had developed an abiding interest in the receptionist at his office. One thing was certain: she was never going to become so dependent on a man again.

Placing a hand on each front corner of the machine, Mike wiggled it back and forth. "Definite list to the right," he said, kneeling again to adjust the screw.

"Jiggle it, see if it's any better," he instructed.

Another half turn brought the appliance to stability, but Mike made no effort to stand up. "Now what?" Angelina asked.

"You have . . . *terrific* legs."

Angelina rolled her eyes in exasperation, but her frown was benign. It was difficult to sustain anger at a man who took such obvious delight in admiring her. "Are we finished?"

"I hope not," Mike said, rising to his feet. Reading her expression, he said, "Oh, you meant with the washing machine? Probably. We just need to fill her up and make sure none of the connections are leaking. You can throw in a load of clothes if you want to."

"Now *there's* an invitation I can't refuse," she said.

A few minutes later Mike inspected the hose connections closely, using the flashlight, and pronounced them watertight. The announcement led into an awkward moment.

"Thanks for...everything," Angelina said. "I'm afraid this hasn't been much of a Saturday night for you."

"It had its moments," he said. "Besides, the evening's still young."

"Not quite," Angelina said.

"We could catch the last showing of a movie," he suggested hopefully.

"I don't think so."

He wrapped his hands loosely around her upper arms. "I'd really like to spend some time with you, get to know you better."

He might as well have pulled her into a torrid embrace, she was that aware of his fingers curved gently around her arms, of his eyes on her face. "Why don't you go home, take two cold showers and call me in a few days if you're still interested."

Lifting his right hand to caress her cheek with his fingertips, he gave her a soft, seductive smile. "Things got a little out of control earlier—"

"A little," Angelina said dryly.

"Hey, look, I admit you have a way of bringing out the beast in me, but we're civilized adults. We ought to be able to spend a little time together without succumbing to our baser urges."

Speak for yourself, Angelina thought. She'd never realized the erogenous-zone potential of the face, but what his slightly rough, infinitely gentle fingertips were doing to her senses was probably illegal in some conservative cultures.

"Come on," he said. "I'll let you pick the movie."

"Maybe another time," she said. *Sometime when you call and invite me ahead of time so I feel like a choice instead of a spontaneous event.*

Hearing the finality in her answer, he shrugged philosophically and let his hands fall to his sides. "How about a walk?" He didn't give her time to voice the refusal she was framing before coaxing, "It'll be good for the puppy."

THE NIGHT WAS perfect for a leisurely stroll—the moon was almost full, the sky cloudless, the air crisply cool. Mike took command of Princess's leash and gave the rambunctious puppy a great deal of freedom, letting her alternate between mad, frolicking dashes and abrupt stops to sniff mailbox posts, light poles and an occasional toad.

Angelina relaxed as they walked, chatting about raising puppies, the "Excellent" Lily got on her report on raccoons and the benefits of living where you could go walking on a February night without having to wear a coat. Nice safe topics. Her mood had mellowed substantially by the time they completed a circuit of the neighborhood streets which brought them back to her house.

Mike took the time to pet and praise the dog after unhooking the leash.

Angelina watched him ruff the dog's neck and dreaded the goodbye which was imminent. The tension that had ebbed during their stroll began creeping back into her muscles, but she forced a smile as he straightened and gave her a self-conscious grin.

He was suffering from a bit of apprehension, too, she realized. She found that fact oddly reassuring.

"Thanks," she said, determined not to let the silence become oppressive. "For delivering the washing machine and dinner and—"

"Uh-uh. I have to thank you for dinner," he said. "The fajitas-for-two special and free dessert, remember?"

"It'll be years before I forget that fried ice cream."

This time, the silence won. Finally, Angelina extended her right hand. "Well—"

He took her hand as if to shake it, but the expression in his eyes and the sensuality in his grin told her it wasn't going to be that easy. Slowly, gently, deliberately, he pulled her hand, forcing her nearer. Near enough to feel the heat of his body. Near enough to hear him breathing. Near enough to smell his after-shave. Near enough to make her lose herself in his kiss.

7

MIKE TRIED not to look at his *Minimum Requirements for a Woman* list as he washed his hands. Reading it only saddled him with a heaping serving of self-loathing for being foolish enough to ignore his own advice.

Ignore it? Hell, he'd done more than ignore it. He'd thumbed his nose at it. One look at Angelina Winters and he'd slipped into the role of gallant knight so fast, it was a wonder he didn't have whiplash from the fall.

And look what had happened . . . what had almost happened . . . what might yet happen . . .

Despite his resolve, his mind dwelled on the pleasant possibilities as he blotted his hands with a paper towel.

"Should I bring in your next patient now?" Suzie asked, poking her head into the utility room.

Mike nodded. "I'm just finishing up here. How stacked up are we?"

Tuesday was not his regular surgery day, but he'd had an emergency that required immediate repair surgery with full anesthesia, and now he was behind in his routine appointments.

"Not too bad," Suzie reported. "I managed to reschedule a couple of late-morning appointments, so you should be able to catch up if you take a short lunch. By the way, there's a delivery at the desk you'll probably want to take a look at."

"It's about time. I ordered that new light weeks ago. I think the medical supply company must be delivering by pack mule these days."

"This isn't a light. And it isn't from the medical supplier," Suzie said in her busybody voice.

Cookies! The thought sprang to mind. Angelina had said she was going to make him some, and he hadn't realized, until this moment, how much he'd been hoping that she would follow through on the plan. "I wonder what kind they are," he said, trailing Suzie down the hall.

Suzie waited until the reception desk was within sight, then stepped aside dramatically and announced, "Pussy willows."

"Pussy willows?" Mike said, temporarily befuddled.

"*Very expensive* pussy willows," Suzie confirmed.

Mike stared in disbelief at the strands of the fuzzytipped branches artfully arranged in an expensivelooking ceramic vase. "This came for me?"

"Uh-huh."

"Who would send me a pot of pussy willows?"

Suzie gave him a quizzical look. "You don't know?"

He shook his head.

"Well, open the card!" Suzie said. "I've been about to expire of sheer curiosity for the past hour."

Mike plucked the envelope from a plastic holder tucked in among the reeds. Espey Gallery was printed on the outside in silver ink. "A gallery, no less."

"One of the ritziest shops in Winter Park," Suzie informed him. Suzie kept up with such things.

"This doesn't make any sense," Mike said, wrestling with the sealed envelope.

"You really *don't* know who sent them, do you?" Suzie asked, surprised.

Mike shrugged. "I haven't the vaguest idea. Some grateful pet owner, I suppose."

"Some *very* grateful pet owner," Suzie speculated. "Whoever sent those dropped a good piece of change. The vase alone is probably in the three digits."

"I'll be damned!"

"Who?" Suzie prompted.

"Samantha Curry," he said, grinning involuntarily. With everything that had happened lately, he'd actually forgotten about Samantha Curry. This was an omen. It must be. A nudge in the right direction to remind him of his resolve. He read the note then looked at Suzie. "She appreciates my volunteering my time last Saturday."

"Well, it's clever. I'll give her that."

"Clever?" Mike asked.

"Pussy willows for a veterinarian."

"Mmm," Mike agreed vaguely, preoccupied with the part of the note he hadn't shared with Suzie. The Espey Gallery was exhibiting sculptures of one of Samantha's college friends and the opening would be a week from Saturday. Would he care to accompany her?

Would a starving man care for a steak? he thought wryly.

That evening, he called Samantha to thank her for the pussy willows and accept the invitation, extending it to include dinner after the cocktail event at the gallery. She suggested a restaurant near the gallery. A French restaurant.

He hung up the phone feeling smug. A gallery opening. A French restaurant. This was good. Very good. He was finally moving away from women like Beth Ann. He'd had a close encounter with potential disaster, but now he was back on track, moving in the right direction. Not that he was out of danger where Angelina Winters was concerned. Despite her money woes and her gamine daughter and the ex-husband she didn't discuss, it was not going to be easy for him to forget those big brown eyes, or the way she lifted her chin defiantly when challenged.

A sigh escaped him. *Those legs. Her smile. The sound of her voice.*

By week's end, he was convinced that the surest way to become obsessed with a woman was to tell yourself you weren't going to think about her. Everything reminded him of Angelina—brown-and-white dogs brought into his office for treatment, little girls the age of Lily, advertisements for Mexican restaurants, *tire commercials*—

He battled the obsession with substitution. When Angelina sprang into his mind, he simply forced himself to think of Samantha Curry instead. It wasn't so difficult. Auburn hair instead of black. A silk blouse instead of a faded T-shirt. And each time he stood at the sink in front of his *Minimum Requirements for a Woman* list, he gloatingly reminded himself that Samantha Curry scored a perfect six, while Angelina rated less than a two. He even wrote it on the list for good measure: Samantha 6. While he was at it, he wrote Angelina above Winters, and went over the one-point-five again with the pen.

Tired of seeing her old washer in his van—the fact that he'd insisted on hauling it away for her only proved that he'd been falling into his old pattern of playing the pushover nice-guy chump—he took it to Suzie's mother-in-law's neighbor, Mr. Peledrino, a retired mechanic from New Jersey who tinkered with old appliances in a shop behind his house.

Mr. Peledrino's Boston terriers, Spike and Spots, dashed out to investigate the van when Mike pulled into the driveway. Mr. Peledrino, bald and potbellied but still spry, was close behind. "Doc," he greeted. "What brings you here?"

"Brought you a washing machine," Mike replied, opening the sliding door of the van.

"Well, let's have a look at it," Mr. Peledrino said. He and both dogs climbed into the van. The dogs sniffed excitedly at the smorgasbord of animal scents in the vehicle as Mr. Peledrino examined the washer. "She's an old one," he said.

"I thought maybe you could salvage some parts from it."

"Maybe," Mr. Peledrino said, standing back now and scratching his chin. "Maybe not. Hard to tell without plugging her in and starting her up. But it's a popular model, and the shell's in pretty good shape. I can give you ten bucks for it."

"Ten bucks?" It hadn't occurred to Mike that Mr. Peledrino would pay for the machine.

"It's my best offer. Take it or leave it. I don't dicker."

Mike poised his mouth to refuse the money, but reconsidered when he realized that Angelina could probably use it. He nodded.

"I pay in checks, not cash," Peledrino said a few minutes later, after they'd moved the washer into the shop. "It discourages thieves from bringing me stolen goods. How do you want this made out?"

"To A. Winters," Mike said.

He'd mail her the check, with a note of explanation. Going to see her would be too risky. If he went to her house, he'd probably look at her legs again. Or into her eyes, which was even more dangerous. A man could look at a woman's legs with a certain degree of detachment, but eyes—what was that old saying? Eyes were the window to the soul? Especially eyes like the ones belonging to Angelina Winters.

Angelina's beautiful dark brown eyes were the only thing he couldn't obliterate from his mind by substitution. In fact, he couldn't remember the color of Samantha Curry's eyes.

"ARE YOU SURE Dr. Mike won't mind if we eat one of his cookies?"

"We've already filled up the box for Dr. Mike," Angelina told her daughter. "These are extras."

"Oh," Lily said, accepting the logic at face value. She lost no time getting one of the disputed cookies from the cooling rack to her mouth. "Chocolate chip is my favorite."

"Everybody likes chocolate-chip cookies."

"I'll bet they're Dr. Mike's favorite." She washed down the cookie with a deep gulp of milk and then set her glass on the table with a thoughtful sigh. "I wish Dr. Mike could come over to get his cookies."

"We're going to mail them, remember? So he'll be surprised."

"You could call him and ask him to come over but not tell him about the cookies," Lily suggested. "Then when he got here, we could yell, 'Surprise!' and show him the cookies."

Angelina looked at Lily's precious face and reflected that motherhood would be simpler if her daughter weren't so clever. "You think that would be fun, huh?"

"Uh-huh," Lily said, slyly reaching for another cookie.

Angelina picked up a cookie, hoping to neutralize the subject with silence. But Lily persisted. "Why can't you call him?"

Angelina chewed her cookie very slowly, stalling until she could come up with an excuse that would appease Lily. She couldn't very well tell her the truth: that Dr. Mike had apparently gone home, taken a cold shower and decided that he wasn't as anxious to get to know her as he'd thought he was when they were necking in the laundry room.

"Dr. Mike is a very busy man," she said finally. "He's been nice enough to come over and do favors for us twice. Now we have to do something special for him."

"But if he came over, then I could see him."

"We're not calling him, and he's not coming over," Angelina said firmly. "You can make him a nice thank-you note to go in the package."

"He could see Princess, too," Lily persisted. "He likes Princess."

"Lily," Angelina warned with motherly menace. Ignoring Lily's aggrieved sigh, she gathered the cookie sheets and carried them to the sink to wash them.

Reaching for the sink stopper, she frowned at the stream of water pouring from the faucet. Tiny acorns became mighty oaks; apparently, tiny drips became constant flows. She was going to have to do something about the problem soon. Exactly what, she wasn't sure, but since she couldn't afford a plumber, she was going to have to find out how to fix the dripping tap herself. They had how-to books for such things.

If only they had manuals on how to forget sexy veterinarians! Or sex in general.

She'd been handling sex—or the lack of it—reasonably well since the divorce. Then she'd met Mike Calder. Now—

It was as though the female need in her had been stored away, bit by bit, accumulating silently until he came along to stir it up. Not since Sleeping Beauty had a single kiss caused such an awakening!

Angelina attacked the baked-on cookie residue with a plastic scrubber. Obviously, Mike Calder was no prince. A knight, maybe, rescuing damsels in distress, but no prince. Princes didn't say they wanted to get to know you and then disappear.

She was just damn glad she hadn't made love with him. At least, the reasonable part of her was glad; certain parts of her weren't as appreciative of her strength of character, and those parts seemed to have a disproportionate influence over her dreams. Maybe if she . . . if they—

She refused to think about it. She couldn't change history, and in light of his propensity to drop out of sight, she was probably better off regretting the lost opportunity than regretting letting him into her bed. After all, it was better to be virtuous and frustrated than foolish and satisfied—at least, it ought to be.

Unfortunately, she seemed to be suffering from the frustration far more acutely than she was benefiting from the virtue.

SHOULDERS REASONABLY broad. Stomach reasonably flat. Legs reasonably long. Hair stylishly cut and still reasonably thick. Shoes polished to a military shine.

All in all, Mike decided, he wasn't such a bad-looking fellow for a thirty-something veterinarian. He rarely preened in front of the mirror, but he even more rarely escorted beautiful heiresses to gallery openings, and he figured it wouldn't hurt to do a little double-checking.

His new suit fit exceptionally well. He'd bought it for Tracy's wedding when the ceremony was going to be a small affair and only the groom was going to wear a tuxedo. He'd just brought it home, with the alterations already done, when his mother called to tell him about the change of plans.

He'd lamented the wasted expenditure at the time, but when Samantha answered her door and he saw how impeccably dressed she was, he was glad he'd had the new suit handy. Her russet linen sheath seemed an artist's extension of her auburn hair, while an exotic brass-and-bronze choker with an Egyptian motif added the perfect touch of drama to the starkly simple dress.

She did not enter the gallery but, rather, made an entrance, drawing eyes and stopping conversation as she made a circuit of the room, dropping kisses on cheeks, introducing Mike to everyone along the way and whispering asides as they moved from person to person.

"Freddy started this gallery single-handedly," she would say aloud, then, as they made their way to the next person, "He has great vision. It's a shame he has no art judgment."

Or, "Willa took the photograph for the Common Pet Sense ball poster last year," then, "It was a perfectly *maudlin* image, but the pathetic puppy was just plebeian enough to appeal to the masses."

Or, "No one plays 'Joy' like Chet," then, "Chet is a divine musician, but I got trapped in a dark hallway with him once and he was all over me. The man is an octopus!"

They paused briefly to study each of the sculptures prominently displayed throughout the room. Samantha's comments ranged from, "God, even Freddy knows better than this. She must be sleeping with him," to, "I've seen better execution at high school art shows," to, "I can't believe she has the audacity to display this in public."

But when they encountered the artist finally, Samantha was all hugs and kissy-kissy with the woman. "Your first opening," she gushed. "You must be delirious with pride."

"Terrified is a more apt description," replied the woman. She was stunning, with jet black hair and alabaster skin. Her formfitting black dress was accented by a white band around the bodice trimmed with a stiff, wide bow that covered one shoulder. The other shoulder, pale and flawless as chalk, was bare.

"Mike, this is my *very* best friend from college, Lizzy. Lizzy, this is Dr. Mike Calder."

After the requisite handshakes and nice-to-meet-yous, Lizzy tilted her head toward Samantha's. "What do you think—really?"

"This show will be the talk of the entire arts community," Samantha replied coolly.

Because he'd been privy to her earlier comments, Mike recognized the cruel irony in Samantha's words. He found it disturbing, but reminded himself that Samantha was in an awkward situation, liking the artist but not liking the art.

"Do you have a specialty, Dr. Calder?" Lizzy asked.

"Small animals," Mike replied.

"Animals?"

"Mike's a veterinarian," Samantha said.

Lizzy gave him a stunning smile. "You must take care of Samantha's Havanas."

"No," he said, giving Samantha a look of surprise. "You have Havanas?" The breed was extremely rare and expensive.

"They're national champions," Lizzy said.

"Not yet," Samantha corrected. "But they're potentials. They're nationally ranked." She draped her arm over Mike's possessively. "I met Mike through my volunteer work with CPS. We haven't had a chance to swap animal stories yet."

They were joined then by Freddy, the gallery owner, and a distinguished-looking gentleman. "Excuse us, please. We don't mean to interrupt, Lizzy, but Dr. Leblanc is anxious to meet you. He's particularly interested in *The Angel on a Cowboy's Shoulder.*"

Lizzy gave them an apologetic shrug and turned to talk to the man. Samantha, her arm still draped over Mike's, guided him away, stopping in front of the next sculpture they came to, which she studied with an artist's intensity.

"Lizzy seems nice," Mike commented.

"Poor Lizzy," Samantha said, stealing a glance at her friend. "That dreadful dress!"

Mike didn't see what was so dreadful about the dress. Lizzy had the figure to fill it out nicely, and every man in the room had noticed it. He refrained from pointing that out, thinking perhaps that was what Samantha found so objectionable.

He was relieved when she suggested they leave the gallery, hoping that the intimacy of a quiet restaurant would give them a chance to talk.

Samantha exited the room the same way she entered it, erect, walking with a finishing-school stride, as if she owned the room and everything and everyone in it. And he was a prop, as ornamental as the tuxedoed escorts at a debutante's ball.

Chez Jacques lived up to his expectations, offering a dimly lit room with candles on the tables and Edith Piaf on the sound system. Between soup, salad and flambéed crepes, they discussed Samantha's involvement with Common Pet Sense.

"You must devote a lot of time to it," Mike said.

"I'm lucky enough to have the time to devote," Samantha replied. "Volunteerism is my career."

"You don't have a job?" he asked, tactlessly blurting out the question in his surprise.

She shrugged. "I considered it after college, but why should I take a job away from someone who needs the income? Besides, a job would be so *dreary*—setting an alarm, and having to show up every day and follow someone else's rules."

Her attitude startled him. For as long as he could recall, he'd wanted to be a veterinarian. His high school years were spent in preparation for college, his college years in preparation for vet school. The burning desire to be a veterinarian had carried him through the challenges and rigors of veterinary courses. He could not imagine the life she described, drifting from social event to volunteer project without the prospect of meeting some personal goal.

"What was your major in college?" he asked, genuinely curious.

"Art," she said. "I have a master's in art history." She smiled. "It's a good thing I *don't* need a job, isn't it? I'd either have to teach, which would be the most dreadful job I could think of, or open a gallery. Although, I suppose having a gallery wouldn't be so bad, discovering and developing new talent."

"Like your friend Freddy?"

"Oh, puh-leeze! Freddy wouldn't know good art if it bit him on his backside," she said. "His gallery is fashionable in the Orlando suburbs, but he'd be laughed out of New York in a minute."

He wanted badly to ask her why she went to the gallery if that's the way she felt about Freddy's aesthetic judgment, but he held back. He knew why she'd gone, and it wasn't about supporting an old college friend. It was about making an entrance, being seen at the right place with the right people, holding her place in a tight social circle.

"So," he said, "tell me about your cats."

She had a pair of the rare cats, both female and both nationally ranked. Neither had ever been bred, although she planned to breed them if they ever won a national championship. "They're magnificent animals," she said. "They're English, so they're the true Havanas, rich chocolate brown. I bought them in England. The American Havanas are much darker. They take their name from the color of good tobacco, you know."

"Actually, I didn't know. I don't think I've ever seen a Havana."

"I'll show them to you when we go back to the house, if you'd like."

"I'd like to see them," Mike said. He found he could muster no real enthusiasm over the invitation into her home. Usually, when he'd spent several hours with a woman, he knew whether or not he'd want to commit himself enough to cross her threshold. But, usually, he selected women through instinct. Chemistry. Visceral reaction. And while he earnestly believed Samantha Curry was motivated by chemistry when she pursued him, he was approaching Samantha Curry through his head instead of through his heart.

She's a perfect six, the perfect woman. It was becoming a litany inside his head. His brain kept talking, but his heart wasn't buying it. Still, determined, he persevered. He crossed the threshold, followed her into a room so stylish, so pristine, so perfect that it showed no trace of human habitation—and no welcoming warmth to comfort a weary human.

Samantha, also pristine and perfect in her elegant linen dress, smiled at him much the way she'd smiled in the sandwich shop, and he saw in her not a woman with whom he could share human warmth and emotion, but a predator luring prey into her lair.

"The *salon des chats* is this way," she said. "I converted a bedroom."

Beyond a brass-framed glass door stretched a wonderland for cats, with high-rise carpeted climbing posts, rings suspended from the ceiling, and dozens of toys and balls to bat about. In the corner, food and water dishes sat in a facsimile sidewalk café, complete with miniature café tables and a striped canopy overhang. A room divider lined with gathered satin held an ornate *Toilette* sign, obviously concealing the litter boxes in the opposite corner.

The feline residents, lounging on the elevated platforms, did not stir as the humans approached. "That's what I love about cats," Mike said. "They're so aloof."

"I could call them," Samantha said, "but I don't really want to go in with my good clothes on. Even though the room is thoroughly vacuumed twice a week, the hair—"

"That's the thing I like second best about cats," Mike said. But it bothered him, that fancy little room where the cats lived and the owner who didn't venture inside for fear of getting hair on her clothes.

The cats' disinterest in their owner's approach also bothered him. He was no sap where animals were concerned, but he couldn't imagine an animal-owner relationship so devoid of interest or affection on either side.

"This is some setup," he said, recognizing the comment to be as duplicitous as the one Samantha had made to her friend earlier.

"Nothing but the best for my darlings," she said. "Although you wouldn't *believe* how hard it is to find someone willing to do litter boxes. My cleaning service charges extra."

"That must be annoying," he said, wondering if she'd even hear the irony.

A long moment passed in silence before Samantha splayed her hand over his forearm. "Why don't I show you *my* room now," she suggested, her voice sultry with innuendo.

The abruptness of the proposition was the only thing that made him hesitate. He wasn't actually considering staying with her, he realized as he studied her face. He was thinking how devoid of warmth her eyes were. There was calculation there, the cruel cunning of an animal on the prowl.

He drew in a breath and released it slowly. "Samantha . . ."

She stiffened visibly, setting her jaw and squaring her shoulders against the rejection while she gathered her wits to respond to it. Finally she said, coolly, "You're not even going to give it a chance?"

"I just don't think we should rush into anything."

She laughed, softly, but haughtily. "I wasn't asking for a lifetime commitment."

Mike shrugged. Maybe that was the problem. Maybe he was just too weary to invest his energy in a liaison that had nowhere to go and no ambition to head anywhere.

Her chin tilted at a defiant angle. "Too bad," she said. "It might have been fun."

He'd never been more relieved to climb into his van and drive away from a place in his life. *So much for the perfect woman, her perfect dress, her perfect house and her perfect cats.*

He was halfway home before he realized that he didn't want to go there. Not yet. He was too cold and empty inside. Too disheartened to settle only for the company of a mellow old dog. He needed human companionship, conversation, emotional connection.

The sports bar Jerry favored was just a few miles up the road. He could go there, see how Jerry's Saturday night was panning out. He'd been there often enough that he'd probably run into someone he knew, even if he missed Jerry.

But a noisy bar didn't appeal to him, either. He wanted—

Stopped at a red light, he stared blankly into the night and gave up the battle he'd been fighting with himself ever since he'd first laid eyes on Angelina Winters. He didn't want a cold, perfect woman, and he didn't want to go to a noisy, smoky bar filled with strangers pretending to know one another.

Loosening the knot of his tie, he opened the top button of his shirt and heaved a sigh of relief at having finally accepted what he really wanted: he wanted a woman with a soft voice and a warm smile that reached her eyes. He wanted to relax in a room designed for living instead of projecting an image, a room where a puppy could cajole a pat on the head from a caring owner. He wanted to put his arms around a woman who felt like a woman when he held her close, who responded like a woman when he kissed her. A busy woman generous enough to spend an afternoon—or a morning—baking cookies to thank a man for a favor.

The light turned green. Mike pressed the accelerator with renewed conviction, knowing now where he was going and accepting why he was headed there. The check for the old washing machine, still tucked under the elastic strap of the window visor, provided him with an excellent excuse to drop in on her unannounced. Who would complain about getting unexpected money?

Heartened by the light shining from her living room windows, Mike parked in front of her house. He took off his coat and laid it across the passenger seat before taking the check from the visor and heading for the door.

He rang the bell and waited, practicing his story in his mind, telling himself he must act casual even as the anticipation of seeing her set his pulse racing.

"Who is it?" came a shouted query from deep within the house.

Mike tensed. Was he imagining the distress he heard in the cry? "It's Mike. Mike Calder. I have—"

"Come on in. And hurry. Please. *I need helllllp!*"

Adrenaline surged through Mike's veins in response to the panic in her voice. She was in danger.

He grabbed the doorknob and twisted. It didn't budge. Frustrated, he shouted, "The door's locked!"

"Key...under the flowerpot," came the muted cry. "Hurry...please—"

Seconds ticked away as he overturned flowerpots, startling lizards but finding no key. Finally, he found it sandwiched between a flowerpot and the clay saucer in which it sat. Getting the key into the lock seemed to take an eternity but, at last, the tumblers clicked, the knob yielded and he was inside the house, rushing like a bull, running blindly, shouting her name for direction.

"The kitchen!" she cried just as he came to the doorway and caught sight of the carnage.

8

"WHAT THE—?" he said.

"Do something!" she cried. She was at the sink, holding an inverted pot over a geyser rising from the faucet, trying to divert the gush of water into the sink. Despite her efforts, water was everywhere—on the floor, the cabinets, dripping from the ceiling, drenching her hair, her face, her clothes.

"We've got to get that water turned off," he said, entering the soggy room. Relief that she was okay hit him like a bag of bricks.

"No fooling?" she said with uncharacteristic sarcasm. Obviously, plumbing crises played hell with her disposition.

"What . . . how did this happen, anyway?"

"I was changing the whatchamacallit," she said, tilting her head toward a package of washers on the counter that sat next to an illustrated how-to manual on plumbing maintenance. "I unscrewed the handle, just the way the directions said, and suddenly—"

"You're supposed to turn off the water before you take the faucet apart," he said.

"I know. I did. It was the first step."

"How?"

"How?"

"How did you turn off the water?"

She gave him an exasperated frown. "I turned the knob, the way I always do. The faucet was still dripping, of course, that's why I wanted to change the thingamajig in the first place, but I didn't think that would make it—"

"Wrong knob, Angel," he said.

"What?"

"You're supposed to turn it off at the source, not at the faucet."

"The source?"

"The shutoff valve. Under the sink, probably."

"Oh," she said. Crestfallen. Soggy. Sexy as sin. "Well, can you—my arms are so tired they're shaking."

"How long have you been holding this like this?" he asked, stepping behind her and putting his hands on the pot near hers, trapping her between his body and the counter. Under drier circumstances, the position would have had great potential.

"Forever," she told him.

"I've got it," he said. "You look for the shutoff valve."

She released the pot and wiggled out under his arm, another physical maneuver with promise. "Under the sink?"

"Uh-huh. Probably against the back wall."

"What does it look like?"

"A handle of some sort. You'll know it if you see it."

She accidently bumped his knee with the corner of the cabinet door. "Sorry!"

Mike twisted his knees away to let the door open. Angelina removed half a dozen bottles of cleaning products and sponges from the cabinet and stuck her head and shoulders inside.

"Can you see anything?" he asked.

From where he stood, the view was excellent. It was amazing how wet denim clung to female flesh, especially when the female inside was on her hands and knees and her backside was in the air.

"I think . . . is it . . . ?" She backed out and looked up at him. "I'm pretty sure I see it, but it's not going to be easy to get to." She pulled out an aerosol can of carpet cleaner and several scrub brushes and disappeared up to her waist into the cabinet again.

A series of bumps and thumps came from within the cavelike opening. "I can't...I'm not sure...my arm isn't long enough—"

Mike couldn't stand it. Spying a dish towel on the counter, he shoved it up, inside the pot. Tentatively, he released the pot, hoping the towel would stanch the geyser somewhat and the weight of the pot would hold it in place. It worked. It probably wouldn't stay in place very long, but with luck, he should be able to get the water cut off before it completely shifted away.

He did a quick survey of the room. *As if a few hundred more gallons of water would make any difference!*

Writing off his pants as a total loss, he knelt on the wet floor and poked his head in the cabinet, where Angelina was straining to reach the knob she'd located. Spotting the knob, he reached for it, but the garbage disposal blocked his access. He pulled his arm back and moved to the other side of the cabinet—the side Angelina was already occupying. Wetness quickly seeped from her wet shirt into his, and he suspected that his sudden warmth was telegraphed to her just as swiftly.

"What did you do about the wa—" She stopped midsentence, then screeched as a loud thunk sounded just above their heads and a torrential shower peppered their legs.

Concentrating on the immediate task, Mike got his hand around the valve handle and twisted. Gradually, the waterfall abated to an occasional drip.

"Thank God!" Angelina said, backing out of the cabinet.

Mike also backed out. "Your life is just a string of exciting Saturday nights, isn't it?"

"It wasn't—until I met you," she said. Surveying the havoc around her, she emitted a dismal sigh and sank from her knees into a sitting position, disregarding the flood on the floor. She looked at Mike. "Your good clothes—you're all wet."

"So are you," he said, blatantly studying the knit molding her breasts.

Involuntarily, she crossed her arms over her chest. Her eyes were large limpid pools, starkly revealing. Mike saw in them vulnerability, but also a smoldering sensuality as her expression changed from utter dismay to curiosity.

"What are you doing here, anyway?" she asked. "Besides rescuing me, I mean."

"Silly question," he said, lowering his mouth to hers.

The kiss was immediately intense, hot, deep, desperate. Mike hadn't been expecting resistance, but her ardor surprised and delighted him. She slid her arms around him, clung to him, stroked his back restlessly, strained against him as if she couldn't get close enough.

Their wet clothing provided little barrier between them as the lushness of her breasts pressed against his chest. Mike debated only a moment before finding the bottom edge of her shirt and slipping his hands inside. Angelina made a mewling sound in her throat as his hands curved caressingly over her bare ribs, and his thumb grazed the underside of her breast.

She tore her mouth away from his with a groan of protest. "Damn!" she said, prolonging the word.

Mike's racing heart skipped a beat as he wondered if he'd pressed his advantage too far. But suddenly she flung her arms around his neck, knocking him backward with her momentum and landing atop him as she dropped urgent kisses on his face.

Mike shifted his leg from its awkward position and they both gasped as her lower body sank between his thighs. "Do you . . . think," he asked in the midst of a renewed barrage of kisses, "that we...might—" He sighed in ecstasy. "Find someplace—" His *ahh* intensified into a feral groan. "A little . . . less . . . wet?"

She paused her nibbling of his neck. "A bed?"

"Excellent suggestion," he said, praying that she wouldn't change her mind between the kitchen and the bedroom.

Once again, she did the unexpected. Grabbing his tie, she yanked it, forcing him to tilt his head upward. She thrust her face an inch above his. "Are you a prepared little Boy Scout?"

"What?" he asked, struggling for breath.

She pulled a face of sheer exasperation. She wasn't breathing too easily, either. Her ribs expanded and contracted under his hands as she drew in and exhaled a ragged breath.

"Prepared," she repeated, looking acutely uncomfortable. "You know. Responsible." Her eyes widened. *"Safe sex,"* she whispered through clenched teeth.

"A condom?" he asked incredulously.

"Yes!"

He chuckled from sheer astonishment. "Yes."

"Show it to me."

"Show it—"

She gave the tie a yank. "I'm not kidding!"

"Yes, ma'am," he said, grinning. Reluctantly withdrawing his hand from her shirt, he thrust it into his pocket, took out his billfold and held up the foil pouch. "Satisfied now?"

"No," she said. "But I'm going to be."

Still holding his tie, she rolled off him and rose, leading him behind her. "Whatever you do," she murmured, "don't drop that envelope."

Reasonably confident now that she clearly wasn't going to have a change of heart, Mike was a compliant captive. When a beautiful woman wanted to make him a love slave, his philosophy was *Que sera, sera*. Not that it had ever actually happened before.

In the bedroom, she simultaneously kissed him and undressed him—or tried to, peeling his shirt down to his wrists and his pants around his ankles. He helped a little, wrestling with the buttons on the cuffs of his shirt and tossing it aside before removing his shoes and socks and stepping out of the pants.

"Your turn," he said, giving her wet, clinging clothing a lascivious once-over.

"Get into bed and close your eyes," she said.

"You don't get . . . *real* kinky, do you?" he asked, with just a twinge of concern.

"I can't take my clothes off in front of you with the lights on," she said, as if explaining something quite simple to someone quite stupid.

"Are you serious?"

"Trust me," she said with a soft, vulnerable sigh. "This isn't all that easy for me."

Mike turned back the bedding and climbed in. "Do I have to pull the covers over my head?"

Angelina's forehead creased in a most intriguing way as she scowled at him. "This isn't going to work if you make fun of me."

"I'll close my eyes." He pointed. "See. They're closed."

"And—"

"*Don't peep*," he said with her.

Listening to her move was strangely erotic: her footsteps on the carpet, the odd rustle as she removed her wet clothing, her breathing, her swallow of determination before she walked to the bed and slipped between the sheets.

She lay beside him, still and silent for almost a full minute before saying softly, "You can open your eyes now."

"And you can breathe again," he said.

She inhaled raggedly, but remained unnaturally still.

"You know," he continued, "if you moved just a little bit this way—"

She moved swiftly, and not just a little bit. Suddenly, she was on top of him, kissing, stroking, squirming sensually and touching him in wild and whimsical ways. Frenzied, insatiable, uninhibited, she made love to him, unabashedly glorying in the pleasure of being with him.

Still perplexed by the swift turn of events that had taken him from the cold calculation of Samantha Curry's proposition to the spontaneous combustion of Angelina Winters's bed, Mike closed his eyes and surrendered himself to the pleasure of her lovemaking.

Her desire, forthright, undisguised, almost unbearably sweet, fueled the desire he'd always felt for her. Soon he was as aroused as she, aroused by the tenderness that survived the urgency of her caresses, the sincerity that surpassed the intensity of her quest for physical appeasement.

Her fingers curved around him, hugged his swollen, aching flesh, making him desire her even more. "Please!" she rasped. "Now."

Seconds later she lowered herself over his sheathed hardness, crying out with a guttural sigh as her body accommodated their joining. Her soft, moist warmth surrounded him and she undulated above him, driven by primal need. Mike stroked and caressed her, cupping her breasts, chafing their peaks with his palms as her movements grew more mindless and desperate. Instinctively, when her release was imminent, he moved his hands lower to cup her bottom and assist her rhythmic rocking.

Finally, she tensed and then, with a lengthy sensual moan, laid her cheek on his chest above his thundering heart. Mike wrapped his arms around her. Anchoring her close, he rolled her under him and sought his own fulfillment, which came with a shattering intensity.

With his head buried between her breasts, he listened to her heart. Angelina soothed his back with gentle strokes and pressed gentle kisses on his temple. *So nurturing, so . . . giving. Samantha Curry would never—*

The incredulity of where he was, who he was with and how he'd gotten there struck him full force. Things like this just never happened to Mike Calder. He was a passably nice-looking, relatively sophisticated single male professional, but he didn't turn down one beautiful woman and go to bed with another the same evening. Women didn't grab him by the necktie and lead him to their bedrooms and make mad, passionate love to him.

"Holy cow!" he said. "Is Lily in bed?"

"No, she's at her father's." She hesitated. "Dr. Calder," she said, obviously wanting to talk, but unable to find the words.

Mike braced his hands on the bed and gingerly lifted his weight off her, then shifted positions to lie beside her.

"Oh. You *do* remember my last name."

The sound she made was not quite a word. Her embarrassment was almost palpable. Finally, she managed to say, "About . . . what just—"

"Just tell me one thing," he said.

Her forehead wrinkled in concentration.

"Are you going to respect me in the morning?" he asked, stifling a chuckle.

She responded with a gasp of outrage and turned onto her side, presenting her back to him.

Mike pushed up on one elbow. "I'll be right back."

Angelina didn't acknowledge Mike's return when he rejoined her in bed a few minutes later. She wanted to let him know she'd enjoyed their lovemaking, but she wasn't sure exactly how to go about expressing herself. The only other man she'd ever been with was the one she'd married at nineteen, so she wasn't exactly experienced in afterglow etiquette. Men didn't like to talk about sex, anyway, if what she'd heard on talk shows was accurate.

Obviously, the man in bed next to her didn't like being ignored, either, because he began drawing circles on her exposed shoulder with his forefinger. Her entire body was still sensitized from their lovemaking, and his touch was like lightning dancing across her skin.

He drew a line from her shoulder to the small of her back, brushing the sheet aside as his hand moved lower.

"You have a great back," he murmured. "You'll have to let me see it sometime when the lights are on."

She rolled onto her back so she could see his face. He was propped up on one elbow, looking at her. He smiled gently, and she returned the smile, tentatively.

"Does this mean you're speaking to me again?" he asked.

"I don't usually..." Her voice trailed off in a sigh as the words eluded her.

Mike cocked an eyebrow and grinned mischievously. "Drag men who turn off your water into your bedroom and have your way with them?" he suggested.

Angelina scowled.

"I'm sure there are a lot of plumbers who'll be disappointed to hear that."

"What are you doing here, anyway?" she asked after a thoughtful pause.

Again, he offered that diabolical lift of eyebrow, and a grin that was positively lewd. "Besides having incredible sex?"

Oh, God, she thought with a sinking feeling, he thinks I'm always . . . aggressive. She had to tell him, explain. That she'd been lonely. That she'd needed to feel desirable again. That having a man's arms around her had been like...like rain after an extended drought. That she wasn't always so—

"If what... *just happened*—" She felt her cheeks flame as words failed her yet again.

"You mean the incredible sex?"

Ignoring him, she went on. "If it should ever...*happen* again—"

"Oh, it's going to happen again," he said, dipping his head to drop a nibbling kiss on her shoulder. "Soon."

She drew in a deep, fortifying breath and released it in a rush. "Well, if it does, I just want you to know that it might not be quite so...*incredible* next time."

"I don't know why you'd think that." The effect of his lips on her skin as he nibbled his way to her neck lent credence to his argument.

She had to force herself to concentrate on the point she was trying to make. "The truth is, this was the first time I...since the divorce...so, naturally, I was a little—"

"Enthusiastic?" He'd found a hitherto undiscovered erogenous zone just beneath her ear.

"Yes," she said in a rush of breath. "So—"

"So, we may have to be a little more creative and take a little more time to get to the same place." He put his mouth close to her ear and whispered intimately, "Sounds like fun to me."

"Mmmmmm," she said, closing her eyes as he kissed his way from her ear to her mouth.

Patient, unhurried and thorough, the kiss lacked the frenzied urgency of their previous kisses; there was an almost arrogant laziness about it, a sense of having all the time in the world to explore, discover and experience.

Gradually their bodies became involved. Arms wrapped, hands soothed, legs entwined, hair chafed smooth skin, soft flesh met firm muscle, all with the same sense of leisurely indulgence.

Pleasure flowed through Angelina like warm oil, lulling and thrilling at the same time. She wondered if she'd forgotten how wonderful such intimacy could be—or if she'd ever even experienced this richness of physical contentment. Perhaps it was just a difference in perception. With Thomas, she'd been a girl, inexperienced and virginal. Thomas had been a boy, randy and full of adolescent cocksureness. Now she was with a man, responding with a woman's emotional and physical needs.

Still, she clung to enough romance to wish that this kiss could go on forever, weaving its magic spell without having to lead to anything more complicated than this soul-soothing pleasure. But he tore his mouth from hers to say raggedly, "I hope you're a prepared little Girl Scout."

Mellowed by the kiss, she didn't immediately understand what he was asking. Then, as comprehension dawned, she said, "No! I don't have any."

He groaned. "No-o-o. Please. Don't tell me that!"

"You don't have any more?"

"I carry a wallet, not a saddlebag."

"Well, I haven't needed them," she explained apologetically.

He hugged her gently. "How did I get so lucky?"

"You turned off my water." She heaved an exaggerated sigh and cuddled closer. "Speaking of which—I need to get after that mess in the kitchen, anyway, before the house floats off its foundation, or something."

"I'll finish the faucet while you mop."

"Now that the water's off, I can finish the faucet. It's so late. You don't have to stay—"

"But I want to stay," he said, nibbling on her earlobe.

"But it's almost midnight, and—"

"That's it," he teased, feigning indignation. "Have your way with me, then throw me out!"

"But we're out of . . . essentials."

"That's what convenience stores are for."

Angelina chuckled. "Convenience stores are where you buy milk for breakfast when you forget to buy it at the supermarket."

"You live a sheltered life, Mrs. Winters."

"Because I don't know where to buy condoms after midnight?"

He kissed the tip of her nose. "Because it didn't occur to you that I would."

9

"WHAT ARE YOU doing?" Holding the sheet firmly around her breasts, Angelina peered over the edge of the bed to punctuate the question with one of those you'd-better-explain-yourself looks mothers were so good at.

Mike had switched on the bedside lamp. Still totally naked, he was down on one knee examining the connection where the headboard joined the side railing of the bed frame. "This joint has worked loose," he said. "I felt it shift when I got up. Haven't you noticed it?"

"It's old," Angelina replied. "I found it at a flea market."

"A little sandpaper and a dose of wood glue will fix this up just fine," he said. "I'll throw some in the van the next time I come over."

"You don't have to do that," Angelina said. "It's always been loose. It's no big deal."

"It'll be a big deal if it gives way during a . . . crucial moment."

Angelina's expression hardened into a frown. She'd moved the bed from the guest room to the master suite when Thomas had moved out, taking their king-size bed with him. One of the reasons she liked it so much was that the sixty years of memories in the old wood weren't hers to contend with. Until now, there had been no "crucial moments" to contend with, either.

"You don't have to bother," she told him. Having a man install her appliances and diddle with her plumbing was one thing, but *gluing* her bed was another.

"It's not a bother."

"I'll take care of it, okay?" she snapped. Too harshly.

"Uh-oh," Mike said, taking a seat on the edge of the bed.

Now what? Angelina despaired silently. "What's that supposed to mean?"

"Let's get it out in the open."

"If you were any more in the open, they'd arrest you!" His presence—large, male and unclothed—so close was disconcerting.

"What's the real reason you don't want me to fix the bed?"

His perceptiveness was almost as unnerving as having him so near her in all his glory. The full ramifications of allowing a man into her bed—her life—suddenly came crashing down on her. "It's just so . . . it's *my* bed."

"Uh-huh. And you can take care of it."

"Yes."

"And how many semesters of wood shop did you take in school?"

"None, but—" Risking slippage with the sheet, she threw up her hands. "How hard can it be to squirt in a few drops of glue?"

"It wouldn't be hard at all," he agreed. "But why not do it right when someone offers to help?"

Angelina sighed dismally. "I don't want you to do it for me. I want to take care of my own problems."

"You couldn't possibly know how much I appreciate that about you," he said, taking her hands in his.

A long silence ensued. Angelina gazed down at his fingers wrapped around hers. She'd always admired his hands; she knew now how loving they could be. It was impossible to look at them and not remember.

"This isn't *just* about my doing a favor for you, is it?" he asked.

"A bed is so . . . personal. It's like you'd be touching me."

"Not exactly," he said. The warmth in his voice drew her eyes to his face. He was smiling. He lifted his right hand to cradle her cheek. "What if I told you that I hope to be spending a lot of time in this bed?"

"I'd be . . . terrified," she said. But even as the apprehension make her go tense, the prospect of having him there with her filled her with tingling, wondrous exhilaration.

He gathered her into his arms. His strength was comforting. She hadn't realized how alone she'd been, how lonely. She loved Lily with all her heart, but there were times when a woman needed to be a woman as well as a mother. She clung to him as he stroked her back in long, loving strokes.

"You aren't any more terrified than I am, Angel."

She swallowed. "You?"

"You don't think it's intimidating being the first man who's been in your bed since your divorce?"

"I guess I hadn't thought about it."

"Take my word for it, it's intimidating. I practically deflowered you."

Angelina laughed softly. "Hardly." Her laughter faded into pensive silence that stretched overlong before she finally said, "I haven't asked you for any commitments."

"That's right," he agreed, hugging her a bit tighter in an instinctive protective response to the tension he felt claiming her body. "You haven't asked. But you made a commitment when you let me get close to you, and I can't ignore that."

Ignore it? He'd been obsessed with the idea ever since Angelina had dropped that bombshell of information. The odds of keeping a relationship casual went down substantially when a man found out he was her first lover in almost two years. Of course, the odds of keeping it casual had plummeted through the floor the instant he'd fallen head over heels in love with her, although he wasn't quite sure when that was.

It might have been when he saw her trying to change her tire, her face smudged with tire black. Or it might have been substantially later—when he walked into her kitchen and saw her standing barefoot at the stove, stirring the sauce for the tetrazzini.

"What happened tonight was mostly my idea, so you don't have to feel—*obligated*," she said.

Her cheek was soft against his chest. He stroked her hair, silky and dark. "What I'm feeling right now is not obligation," he crooned. "I hate to have to tell you this, but since I *am* a gentleman, I don't have any choice. Your . . . uh, sheet is slipping."

With a soft gasp, she pulled away and yanked the sheet back up over her breasts.

It was everything Mike could do to refrain from tackling her and kissing her until she forgot all about holding on to that ridiculous cover, but they weren't prepared for what would happen if he did. Instead, he grinned charmingly. "Next time I'm going to peek!"

"JUST IN TIME!" Mike said as Angelina exited the bathroom in the master suite, where she had retreated for a shower after finishing the kitchen cleanup.

"For what?" Angelina asked.

"You can find me a couple of magazines to—" His concentration on the repair job he was doing was entirely shot as he looked up from his work and saw her standing there. Fresh from her shower, with her hair loose and fluffy from blow-drying, she was wearing a floor-length robe of emerald green that clung to her curves and shimmered with her every motion.

Although his frankly sensual once-over made her feel a bit self-conscious, Angelina gave him a tentative smile. Having a man look at her as though she were an ice-cream sundae with a bright red cherry on top did wonders for her ego.

"To . . . ?" she prompted.

"Huh?"

"You needed magazines?"

"To...uh, wedge up underneath here and hold this side rail in place. I've got it clamped, but a little extra support never hurts."

"I'll see what I can find," she said. "They're ... uh—" his sensuous gaze was getting a little disconcerting "—in the living room."

His grin was pure sin. "Hurry back, Angel."

She fetched the magazines and helped him wedge the clamped joint.

"That ought to take care of it," he said. "In twelve hours it'll be as good as new." He rose, dusted the knees of his jeans and turned his attention to Angelina. "Now, on to more important things."

Angelina cocked her head coquettishly. "What more important things?"

The question was superfluous. The glint in his eyes left little room for doubt about what he had on his mind. After taking care of the drip in her faucet, he'd made a quick run to his house for dry clothes, tools and more foil envelopes. He was wearing the clothes, he was finished with the tools and now—

"I'm open to suggestion," he said, tracing the curve of her cheek with his forefinger.

"I have a rocking chair with a loose rung," she said sweetly.

He thrust his fingers into her hair, curving his fingers around her scalp. "My clamp is already engaged."

"There's a loose tile in the shower stall," she cooed.

"No grout," he said, slipping his arm around her waist.

"The, uh—" She flicked her tongue across her lips. She hadn't flirted since her first year in college and she found it exhilarating. "Window over the sink sticks."

Abruptly, he tightened his arm, pulling her against him, and coaxed her head back with a gentle tug on her hair. "If I thought you were serious, I'd strangle you."

"I thought you liked fixing things."

"I do," he said, dipping his head to press his forehead against hers. "But it's your turn to fix something for me."

Breathless. Knowing what he meant. Wondering how he'd express it. Waiting. Loving the anticipation. "What?"

His mouth touched hers with the tremulous flitting of a hummingbird's wings. "This."

With a sound that was half sigh, half gasp, Angelina threw her head back as he kissed his way to her neck.

"You smell good. Like a girl," he said huskily.

"As . . . opposed to . . . a shaggy dog?" she asked, although her breathlessness softened what might otherwise have been sharp wit.

"As opposed to—" He finished with a groan as he encountered the V formed by the crisscrossing fronts of her robe. He took his arm from around her waist to part them, brushing the left panel aside, exposing the top of her breast. "Anything else on earth."

He shoved the robe down over her shoulders, exposing her breasts, and stared boldly at the flesh he'd bared.

His admiration did all the magic things an adoring look was supposed to do. Angelina's knees suddenly felt rubbery, her heart raced and heat curled through her body.

"Told you I'd peek," he said with a sexy smile.

"Please," she whispered, unsure what she was asking in the plaintive plea.

"That's not all I'm going to do," he said, gently curving his hand over her left breast and chafing it with his palm.

Angelina watched, fascinated, exhaling a languid sigh as the heat inside her raged into an inferno of yearning. She placed her hands on his shoulders for support as her knees threatened to buckle.

He bowed his head to hers for a claiming kiss while his hand kneaded her aroused flesh. She folded her arms around his neck and pressed her body into his. The silky robe was so thin, like tissue paper between them. His heat, his hardness and his strength excited her.

He tore his mouth from hers and said hoarsely, "I should have waited until morning to fix the bed."

With that, he grasped the comforter and flung it onto the floor.

"What are you doing?" Angelina asked, as shocked by the abrupt end to the kiss as by the absurdity of his actions.

"Improvising," he said, tossing the pillows atop the crumpled comforter.

"OH-H-H," Angelina groaned.

Mike opened one eye. "Is that a sound of passion?"

Angelina stretched the full length of her body to work out the kinks. "It's pain."

"Are you always this grouchy in the morning?"

"Only when I sleep on the floor."

"Such ingratitude, after I fixed your bed."

"I didn't ask you to fix my bed. I didn't even want you to fix my bed, but you *insisted*."

"It was falling apart."

She yawned. "And then you kept me awake half the night."

"Is that a complaint?"

Angelina snuggled up against him. "I really *would* be an ingrate if I complained about *that*."

An involuntary smile claimed her face as she recalled their lovemaking on the makeshift pallet. Her aches were due as much to the hardness of the man next to her as to the hardness of the floor. He'd made love to her thoroughly and well, and she knew it. It scared her a little. A steamy shower would leech the soreness from her body and wash away the scent of him, but the memories of the pleasure they'd shared would not be purged from her mind as handily.

Her first affair. So far it had been all thrills and surprises and physical gratification, with a twist of magic thrown in, but it was new territory for her, both emotionally and socially. She couldn't help feeling a little apprehension over the possible repercussions an affair would have on her already complicated life.

It hadn't been easy replacing a man who brought home a respectable paycheck with a job that barely paid her enough to cover the necessities *if* she could avoid unforeseen circumstances like bald tires and worn-out washing machines, but in the past few months, she'd finally managed to establish a routine and restore some equilibrium to her life. She was managing, finally, and feeling good about herself because of it. She didn't want anything to mess that up now, especially a man.

"Can you see the clock?" she asked. "What time is it?"

"Almost ten," he said, checking his watch instead of the clock. Angelina was pretty sure it was the only thing he was wearing, but it was one item more than she had on.

"It can't be!" she said. "I never sleep past eight o'clock."

"Great sex does that for you," he teased, draping an arm across her and pulling her back up against his chest.

Angelina sighed from sheer pleasure, wishing they could freeze the moment and isolate it from past or future. She liked having his arms around her, liked the illusion of security his strength created. If only this mellow afterglow came with guarantees instead of uncertainty and the potential for heartbreak and disappointment.

She was already in way too deep. What if he turned out to be a jerk, or if she found out he had a wife and three kids? She didn't have the emotional stamina to deal with that kind of disaster. And there was Lily to consider. She didn't want her daughter hurt by any mistakes she made in her own personal life.

"So what are we doing today?" he asked, pressing his lips to her temple. "Want to find brunch somewhere?"

"No. I . . . Lily will be home after lunch, and I like to spend time with her after she's been away."

"The three of us could do something together. Something she'd enjoy."

Suddenly, the floor was hard beneath her hip. Angelina rolled onto her back and turned her head so she could see his face. She forced what she hoped was a cheerful smile. "You have your choice between French toast or homemade waffles, Dr. Calder, and then I'm kicking you out."

"What—did I snore?" he quipped.

She answered him with silence.

"Want to tell me why?"

"This is all new to me. I need some time and space to deal with everything before Lily gets home, and I don't want to bring her into this just yet."

"Into *this*?"

"I don't know how she's going to react to you."

"She adores me," he said. "I'm her raccoon reference."

"She adores you *as* her raccoon reference. But I don't know how she's going to react to my . . . to you and me . . . and I don't think the Sunday after she gets back from a weekend with her father is a good time to spring a new idea on her."

Don't ask! a protective instinct screamed in Mike's head. *She's given you an escape hatch. You don't want to know about the problems with her daughter and her ex-husband.*

A shaft of light from the window above them landed in her dark hair, making it glisten. He knew how soft her hair was, what it felt like against his skin, the way it slipped between his fingers like liquid. "Does she . . . is there a problem with her father?"

She tensed. A long moment of contemplative silence passed before she replied, "She loves her father. It's his stepsons she has a problem with."

"He's remarried?"

She sighed drearily. "His primary objective in leaving me was marrying the woman he left me for."

"He's a fool."

"Lily had a hard enough time trying to understand why her father would go away without her. But when she realized two strange children—two *boys*—were living with him, she felt like she'd been thrown away. Because she was a *girl*."

"Poor kid."

"She's a houseguest in her father's house, and the boys live there. She's over the shock now, but she's always a little subdued when she comes home."

"It's a lot for a child to understand."

"It's a lot for an adult," Angelina said softly.

"Are you—" He exhaled heavily. "I can't believe I'm asking this, but do you still . . . is that why—"

"I'm not pining after him, if that's what you want to know. That's not why I haven't . . ."

She paused to gather her thoughts. "He was my first true love. Looking back on it, I can see that we had been growing apart for some time and I . . . I guess I just chose not to recognize it. I thought it was normal, that it happened to all couples and they just lived with it because they were married. In my family, marriage was forever."

"Things would sure be simpler if it worked that way."

Angelina's forehead creased. "Especially for the children. I can forgive him for finding another woman, but I'll never be able to forgive him for what he's done to Lily."

"Maybe as she gets to know her stepbrothers—"

"Things have eased a bit since her half brother was born."

"Your ex and his wife have a baby?"

Angelina grew very still, and when she spoke, her words were measured and controlled. "It was the cruelest betrayal. I wanted more children. I'd been pressuring him to start another baby when—"

She exhaled heavily. "Well, I guess we know why he was stalling."

She rolled onto her side and drove her fist into the pillow. "For him to have a baby with her, when she already had two children, and my clock was ticking away—"

He ran his forefinger down her arm from the shoulder to the elbow. "Your clock's not ticking all that fast, is it? You have plenty of time. Years."

She rotated her head to look at him. "It's not that simple."

Why not? he wanted to ask and, as if she'd read his mind, she answered the unspoken question. "There's more than just fertility involved."

She might as well have split open his chest and crawled inside his heart; her yearning for a child and a traditional home was almost palpable, and it so clearly mirrored his own frustrated longings. It took every modicum of restraint he could gather to keep from pulling her under him and begging her to make love with him without protection, to let him give her a baby—

His baby.

Their baby. He could picture them as a family. It would work. He, Angelina, Lily, a baby. As many babies as she wanted. He could afford a big family. It would make all those years of studying mean something more than a shingle on the side of a building with his name on it if he had kids to take care of and a wife to come home to every night, to grow old with.

Not just a wife, he amended automatically. Angelina.

"At least this way, Lily has a brother," Angelina said, oblivious to his musings. God, she would think he was certifiably insane if she could read his thoughts!

"She likes the baby. She helps take care of him," Angelina continued. "It gives her something to focus on besides being the odd kid out with her stepmother's boys."

A prolonged silence followed. Finally, she pushed herself up on one elbow. "So what'll it be—French toast or waffles?"

"I'm a waffle man," he said. "But—"

He left the thought hanging until, a moment later, she prompted, "But what?"

"How do you feel about appetizers?" he said. "Before breakfast?"

He grinned with unmistakable intent. "The appetizer I have in mind is a perfect prelude to breakfast in bed."

"Who said anything about breakfast in bed?" she asked. "I said I'd cook. I didn't say I'd serve it in bed."

He guided her onto her back and rolled until his body was pressing down on hers. "That's all right. Just to show you what a nice, agreeable fellow I am, you can have the appetizer anyway."

Her voice took on a sultry quality as her gaze met his. "What if I'm not hungry?"

"You will be," he answered, lowering his mouth to hers.

10

ANGELINA WAS NOWHERE in sight when Mike entered the print shop. A young man digging into the guts of a sizable copy machine which sat against one wall looked up long enough to say, "I'll be right with you."

The man pulled a crumpled sheet of paper from the paper path and wadded it into a ball, then snapped the machine closed. Turning to the woman who'd been making copies, he said, "It should work now. Just wait until this green ready light comes back on."

The woman nodded, and the young man walked around the counter and directed his attention to Mike. "What can I help you with?"

"I'm looking for Mrs. Winters. I need to talk to her about a print job."

"Mrs. Winters?" the young man asked. "Oh. You mean Angelina. She's probably in her cubicle. I'll tell her someone wants to see her."

He disappeared through a door leading into the interior of the building and reappeared a few seconds later. "She'll be right out."

It was worth the trouble of driving to the shop to see her face light up when she walked through the doorway and saw him. "Mike!" she said. "What are you doing here?"

"I hope it's not a bad time," he said. "I need your help. Professionally."

She gave a small shrug. "Well, come on back. Step into my office."

He followed her past a printing press, where a pressman was feeding stacks of glossy paper into the jaws of an ominous-looking, noisy machine, to a small cubicle equipped with a desk, computer and laser printer. An aging work counter held a set of In and Out trays, looseleaf clip-art books in tall plastic binders and a plastic utility basket filled with scissors, glue stick, liquid correction fluid and a couple of paper-cutting knives with wicked-looking blades. "So this is where you work," he said.

"It's more like a cubbyhole than an office, but at least there's a window."

Grinning, he reached for Angelina's hand. "How private is it?"

"Private enough for a kiss, if we stay away from the door," she said, smiling slyly. "Harvey—that's the pressman—can't see around corners."

"Works for me," Mike said, taking a step backward and pulling her with him.

The kiss was short and sweet. Chuckling softly, Angelina wiped a smudge of lipstick from his lip with her thumb. She lifted an eyebrow inquisitively. "What was it you were saying about needing my help?"

"It's a favor for my sister."

"Have a seat," she suggested, gesturing to a molded plastic chair. She settled into the chair behind her desk. "What kind of favor?"

"Wedding announcements," he replied, releasing a small sigh of bewilderment. "My sister's getting married in a few weeks and since my father's deceased, I'm giving the bride away."

"And she wants you to take care of the wedding announcements?"

"That's about the size of it. She called me this morning in hysterics. She and her fiancé are both going to school in Gainesville, so they decided to have the wedding there because so many of their friends are also in school. Anyway, my mother has decided that since they weren't getting married in our hometown and so many of *her* friends and older relatives can't make the trip, she'd like to send out announcements."

"Announcements are so . . . personal," Angelina said. "Doesn't your sister want to—"

"My sister's in vet school, and it's a rough semester. She and Josh just wanted a small, simple ceremony with close friends and family. They didn't want formal invitations, much less formal announcements. My sister just wants to placate Mother."

"Then your mother—"

"She insisted that the bride and groom pick them out. We're, uh, going to fudge a little. I'm sending them to Tracy, and she'll forward them to Mother. I have all the information, names and the date and place." He gave her a winning smile. "I told Tracy I had a friend who'd know just what she needed."

Angelina contemplated the challenge a moment. "You'll have to pick out the card before I can set the type. Did she give you any suggestions?"

"She said to look for something with hearts."

"Something with hearts," she mused aloud. "I think I know just the one. It's called Tumbling Hearts. The sample books are out front. I'll show you."

"It's nice," Mike said a few minutes later, when she pointed out the trifold card with embossed hearts along the edges which overlapped when the card was folded. "I think Tracy will like it."

"The hearts come in sweetheart pink, buttercream yellow or ice blue. Does your sister have a color preference?"

"The bridesmaids are wearing pink," Mike said.

"Pink it is, then," Angelina said, taking an order pad from behind the counter. "There's a minimum order of fifty, with increments of twenty-five." Her forehead crinkled. "Did I say something funny?"

"I've just never seen you in business mode before," he said. "You're very efficient."

She shrugged away the compliment. "I do this all the time. Although, I must say, the last thing I expected today was to be picking out wedding announcements with you."

She must have seen how off guard the remark caught him, because she said, somewhat sharply, "That was a joke. You can breathe again."

"It wasn't that," he said. "It was . . . this whole wedding business gets on my nerves. Weddings in general make me edgy."

"Well, that explains why an eligible bachelor like you has remained eligible for so long."

If only you knew, Mike thought, realizing that he was going to have to tell her all about his close encounter with matrimony soon.

"Do you want to look at typefaces, or do you want me to choose one?"

"I trust your judgment."

She nodded. "I'll use something flowing and delicate."

"Have you mentioned the zoo trip to Lily?" he asked as she filled out the order blank.

After much discussion, she had finally agreed that they could go on an outing and include Lily. Mike had suggested the zoo because of Lily's affection for animals.

"She's looking forward to it."

"What did she say about my coming along?"

"She said you ought to be able to tell her all about the animals. How many announcements do you need?"

"A hundred and fifty. Can we finish this in your office?"

"That depends."

"On what?"

"On whether or not you have ulterior motives unrelated to your sister's wedding announcements."

"I most certainly do have an ulterior motive," he said. "I want to kiss you within an inch of your life."

"I was hoping you'd say that," she said, smiling brightly. "Follow me, sir."

Mike loved her so much at that moment that he almost shouted it.

THE CENTRAL FLORIDA ZOO was small but more than adequate to excite and fuel the imagination of a seven-year-old, especially a seven-year-old who had a personal guide to provide fascinating information about each animal.

Especially a seven-year-old girl who felt as though she'd been ousted from her father's life and was hungry for daddy-like attention. Angelina observed the bond developing between Lily and Mike almost as though it were a physical linking instead of an emotional one.

Mike did all the "daddy" things. He lifted Lily to his shoulders when height gave her a better vantage point. He made a growling sound and poked Lily in the ribs when she was staring spellbound at a bear. He mimicked a monkey as they stood in front of the monkey cages. He helped Lily pronounce the English and Latin animal names posted on the signs marking each exhibit. He bought special food pellets for her to feed the animals in the petting pen, then he dashed into the gift shop for a disposable camera so he could photograph Lily with the goats and llamas and the tame crow who begged for food. On the way out of the park, he dropped quarters into one vending machine after another so Lily could "make" plastic models of the animals she'd seen.

While Lily left the zoo exhilarated, with an armful of souvenirs, Angelina left with a heart full of conflicting emotions. She was glad of his rapport with Lily, and yet she was also terrified of it. What if Lily grew attached to him and he suddenly disappeared from her life because it didn't work out between him and Angelina? It wasn't fair to her daughter to put the child's emotional health in such jeopardy.

And what if you get attached to him and he suddenly disappears? she asked herself. Her own risk of getting hurt was as great as Lily's, if not greater.

But you're an adult. You understand the situation. You have a choice whether to take the chance. Lily doesn't.

And the more time she spent with Mike, the more she realized that her risk was indeed great. She could so easily fall in love with him. Because, even as he did all the "daddy" things with Lily, he was doing all the "lover" things with Angelina. Secret glances. Knowing smiles. Furtive touches that seemed innocent but held the promise of much more. Looks that said, "Wait until we're alone."

No one said it would be easy, she thought. It wasn't fair, either. She'd never planned on being divorced, or having all the problems single motherhood presented.

"Zoos always make me hungry," Mike announced in the car. "But it's too early for dinner, so I'll have to settle for ice cream. How about you, Lily? Does the zoo make you hungry for ice cream?"

"Yeah!" Lily said with such a note of awe that an observer would think she hadn't had ice cream in at least five years.

It was settled before they went into the ice-cream parlor that Lily would get a double-decker cone with a scoop of both caramel turtle and bubble-gum ice cream. Mike went to the counter to order, and Angelina herded Lily into the bathroom to wash the billy goat and llama germs off her hands. Mike was still waiting his turn in line when they returned to the dining area.

"You guys go ahead and find a table," he suggested.

Lily chose a booth and slid in across from Angelina. She propped her elbow on the table and sighed so forcefully that her entire body vibrated. "Mommy?"

"What, sweetie?" Angelina asked, her maternal instinct piqued by the gravity in the way her daughter had said the word.

"You know how you said that sometimes after people got divorced they met people and fell in love and that's how come I got a stepmother? Because Daddy married Denise?"

"Yes, sweetie," Angelina replied, trying not to let her apprehension show. She had a sinking feeling that she knew exactly where the conversation was headed.

"Denise was a mommy when she fell in love with Daddy, wasn't she?"

"Yes, she was. She was Timmy and Morgan's mommy."

Lily's lips compressed as she mentally linked ideas.

"Then sometimes mommies fall in love, too, just like daddies?"

"That's the way it works."

Lily hesitated a long time before asking, "Are you going to fall in love?"

Well, there it is, Angelina thought. She tried to answer as though the question were no more significant than the dozens of other questions Lily asked her every day. "I might, if I met the right man."

"And then I'd have a new daddy?"

"Well, if I got married, you would." She let Lily ponder her answer a while before asking, "What would you think about that?"

It seemed like a very long time passed before Lily sighed and replied, "It would be okay, I guess. As long as he was nice."

"As long as who was nice?" Mike asked, passing out ice-cream cones.

"My new daddy," Lily said.

Mike took three seconds too long to cover his initial reaction. Sliding onto the bench next to Lily, he said, "Are you going to get a new daddy?"

He cast Angelina a curious look while Lily took what seemed like an inordinate amount of time licking her ice cream before saying matter-of-factly, "I will if Mommy gets married again."

"Quick, Lily! The other side of the cone!" Angelina said, silently giving thanks for ice-cream drips, even as she flashed Mike a look that said they'd discuss it later. For the time being, the subject was dropped while they speculated whether Lily could really eat two whole scoops and whether caramel turtle was really the most delicious flavor of all time.

ANGELINA'S FIRST opportunity to introduce the subject again was after she'd returned to the living room after tucking Lily in bed for the night. "She's got all her plastic animals lined up beside her under the covers," she told Mike.

"I'm glad she enjoyed the zoo."

"Why wouldn't she, when she had her own private guide?"

"She's so interested in animals," he said. "She soaks up information like a sponge."

"That's the way seven-year-olds are," Angelina said. "You were great with her, by the way."

"I loved it as much as she did."

"I know." She grew very still. "Mike . . ."

"What's this I hear about your getting married, Mrs. Winters?" he asked dryly.

Angelina frowned. "Lily's still working all this divorce and marriage stuff out in her mind. When she brought up the idea of my getting married, it was . . . it *wasn't* anything I said. It was—"

"And here I thought you'd told her to size me up for daddy potential."

"Please don't joke about this."

"I've dated women with children before. Don't you think I realize that kids come up with things on their own?"

"I don't even think she picked up on anything between you and me. I think it was sheer . . . opportunism."

"You're going to have to explain that one," he said.

"Lily lost most of the advantages of having a father when Thomas moved out. And to be perfectly frank, she didn't gain much when he married his second wife. It's not as though she got a second mother who adored her. She got a harried stepmother who tolerates her."

She paused to catch her breath. "On the other hand, her stepmother's boys got all the advantages Lily lost. They have her daddy full-time now, while she's only a visitor. Today—from Lily's perspective, it was like having a daddy again, and it must have occurred to her that if I...well, that if a man came into our lives, she'd be the one getting the attention. I don't think it had ever occurred to her before that I might...bring a new man into our situation."

"You've never discussed the possibility with her?" he asked.

Angelina shook her head. "I didn't see any reason to. She's had enough on her mind without the prospect of another major change hanging over her head. And frankly, I didn't expect—"

She was conscious suddenly of his eyes on her face, of his thoughts far removed from the subject under discussion.

"I haven't kissed you all day," he said.

"Oh, Mike," she said, desolate because she wanted so badly to have his arms around her, but sure that they needed to deal with the issue of Lily and how their relationship might affect her before getting distracted.

But she didn't draw away as he leaned forward, didn't stop him from putting his arms around her, didn't resist as his mouth joined hers. Instead, she leaned toward him, slid her fingers into his hair, parted her lips under his.

Reason and purpose fled from her mind. There was just Mike and pleasure and magic.

"Mommy?"

Angelina leapt guiltily away from Mike and stared dazedly at her daughter. Lily, angelic in her mermaid-print nightie, stared back with large sleepy eyes.

Gradually, Lily's eyes became less sleepy and narrowed in suspicion. "You're kissing my mommy," she told Mike incredulously.

"Yes, I am," Mike said.

"Why?" Intense curiosity.

"Because I like her."

Lily's face screwed up in concentration. "Oh."

Angelina recovered enough from the surprise of the situation to ask, "What is it, sweetie? I thought you'd be asleep by now."

Lily pouted sheepishly. "I want Dr. Mike to tuck me in."

Angelina raised an eyebrow as her gaze met Mike's.

"I just happen to be an expert tucker-inner," Mike said. "But I do have rules, and one of them is that I couldn't possibly tuck a little girl in unless she rides piggyback to bed."

"I can ride piggyback!"

Chuckling, Mike rose, then knelt in front of Lily. "Well, then, hop aboard, Miss Piggy!"

Angelina listened to the music of her daughter's giggles as Mike carried her out of the room on his back. Then she was left in sudden silence to contemplate the significance of her daughter's wanting Mike to tuck her in.

She was still immersed in deep thought when Mike returned to the living room a few minutes later. Sensing her mood, he sat down next to her on the sofa and wrapped his hand around hers.

"Did she say anything about . . . us?" she asked after a while.

"Not a word. She seemed okay with it."

"We made a mistake bringing her into this," she said.

"We were kissing. People kiss all the time."

"*I* don't kiss men all the time. But I'm not talking about that. I'm talking about . . . the zoo and the ice cream and the cozy little dinner we had and the walk we took with the dog."

"I don't understand," Mike said. Usually, women were grateful that he treated their children like real people. From what he'd gathered, most men behaved as if children carried bubonic plague. "I thought we got along famously."

"Famously," Angelina said.

Mike harrumphed his disbelief. "You can't be jealous!"

"Don't be ridiculous! It makes me feel good all over to see her so relaxed and happy, but it frightens me, too."

"Pardon me for being dense—"

"I don't want her hurt!" Angelina said intently. "I don't want to give her something and then take it away from her."

"We took her to the zoo," he said.

"It was too much like a *family* day," she said. "Mike, her heart is wide open. We're too . . . *new* to be giving her the impression that we can be a happy little family. She doesn't understand that things between men and women are ten times as likely to fall apart as to last."

A frown slowly formed on Mike's mouth as he thought over what she'd said. "Ten to one? Those are heavy odds. Do you think our relationship is that tenuous?"

Angelina's face crumpled into an expression of total bewilderment. "How am I supposed to know? I met my husband when I was eighteen years old, and you're my first affair."

He grasped her shoulders gently. "I don't think the odds are all that heavy."

He saw the panic in her eyes. And the vulnerability. "When you look at me, or touch me," she said, "I'm so . . . awed . . . that I want the fairy-tale ending. I want to believe that it's . . . predestined, and that it'll go on forever. But when I'm . . . when we're not . . . I know it doesn't make any sense to expect it to be any more than a pleasant interlude."

"It's already more than that."

"Yes, but—how do we know what to expect? We could be like—"

She threw up her hands in frustration over not being able to express herself succinctly. "We could be just an illusion. A trick of lights, a diversion or a sleight of hand that makes everyone ooh and aah and then—"

Her eyes narrowed with intensity. "If what we have isn't . . . forever, if it turns out to be an illusion, then I don't want Lily bitter and hurt. I don't want her thinking that she can't trust adults. So, from now on, what we do together will have to be on my time, and not the time I usually give to Lily."

"And if they overlap occasionally?"

"Then they overlap. I just don't think that it's in Lily's best interests for the two of us to plan special things for her as if—"

Concern for her daughter was etched in her face. Mike loved her for that concern, for the unselfishness in her character that implored her to put her daughter's needs first. "Are we on your time now?"

She exhaled softly. "More or less. But Lily's already found us kissing, and I wouldn't be comfortable...I wouldn't want to risk her discovering us in any situation that would raise even more questions in her mind."

Mike frowned. "I take it we won't be retiring to your bedroom."

"Not with Lily across the hall."

"Too bad. I was hoping to make love to you so passionately that the neighbors three houses down would hear your cries of ecstasy."

"Mi-ike!" she whispered, breaking the word into two syllables and rolling her eyes.

"No one's listening," he whispered.

"I am!"

Chuckling, Mike said, "Well, if that's out, how about coming over here and cuddling up next to me a while. I've got some things I want to say to you."

"Like what?" she said, settling her cheek against his chest as his arms encircled her.

"Like the fact that I don't want to see your daughter hurt any more than you do."

She murmured a contented, "Mmm."

"I'll respect your concern, and we won't rush anything. We'll keep *us* between *us* until you're comfortable easing Lily into the idea."

A mellow silence followed. Mike rested his chin on her head, relishing the richness of having her next to him. "Aside from your bed, I can't think of anywhere else on earth I'd rather be right now than right here, holding you like this," he said.

"It feels so good it's scary," she replied softly.

After another silence rich with contentment, Mike said, "I'm not promiscuous, Angelina, but I've had my share of experience. The whole man-woman thing is a crapshoot at best, a long, convoluted process of trial and error. God knows I've tried, and I've damn sure erred."

His arms tightened around her. "All that trial and error gives a man perspective, Angelina. Especially the error part. But it feels right with you. Different. I think it could work for us."

She tilted her head back until her eyes met his beseechingly. "I want that to be true so badly that I don't trust myself to know whether or not I should believe you."

"Believe me," he said, and sealed the pledge with a kiss.

11

ANGELINA GLANCED at the kitchen clock as she dashed to the ringing phone. Nine-thirty. The movie Lily and three of her friends were watching would be over soon, and Angelina wanted to be around to keep the high jinks to a minimum while the videotape was rewinding, so she hoped the call wouldn't be a long one or involve anything too complicated.

"Sorry to call so late, but—"

"Mike?" She was delighted to hear his voice.

"I know I'm on Lily's time, but I have an emergency, and I . . ." She heard him exhale. "Do you know how to sew?"

"You don't want me to stitch up anything alive, do you?"

The sound of his laughter was rich, even through the telephone receiver. "Inanimate, I assure you. It's the tux."

"For your sister's wedding."

"Yes. I picked it up at the mall on the way home and decided to try it on. And the pants . . . well, let's just say that if I bend over, I could get arrested."

"I see."

"The rental shop is closed and I have to leave for Gainesville first thing in the morning." He paused, obviously waiting for her to say something, but she remained silent. Finally, he said, "Can you fix them?"

"I'd have to look at the seam. If the stitching's come loose, it'll be easy. If it's a rip or a tear . . . I'll just have to see it."

"I could bring them over now. If you're not too busy."

A cacophony of little-girl giggles punctuated by the puppy's bark signaled the end of the movie. "I'm not too busy," she said. "Bring them over."

She managed to get the girls settled down in front of another movie with a bowl of popcorn by the time Mike rang the doorbell.

"Who's that?" Lily said.

"It's Dr. Mike," Angelina said on her way to the door. "He has something he wants me to sew for him."

"What?" Lily said, running to the entryway to greet Mike.

"A pair of pants."

Angelina opened the door. Mike entered, and Lily rushed him with a bear hug.

"I'd better take those," Angelina said, rescuing the pinstriped trousers he held neatly draped over a wooden hanger. "Lily, at least let Dr. Mike get inside the house before you knock him over."

"Are those the pants you want Mommy to sew?" Lily asked.

Mike nodded, and Lily giggled. "What kind of pants are they?"

"They're part of a tuxedo," Angelina answered for him. "That's a fancy suit men wear at weddings."

Lily's jaw dropped momentarily. "Are you getting *married?*"

Mike chuckled good-naturedly. "No, sweetheart. My sister's getting married. I'm just giving the bride away."

Angelina opened the waistband of the pants and examined the inside seams.

"What do you think?" Mike asked anxiously.

Angelina put her hands inside the pants and spread her fingers, revealing a gaping slit in the center. "I think if you wear these, you'll catch cold."

"Catch cold!" Lily said with a giggle.

Mike's mouth hardened in exasperation briefly before he said, "What's the prognosis?"

"The stitching has come out," Angelina said. "All that cleaning and pressing wears out the thread."

"Is it fixable?"

"I just have to run it through the machine."

"Thank goodness," Mike said, visibly relieved.

"Princess can shake hands now," Lily told him, cradling the dog in her arms as she and her friends surrounded Mike.

"She can?" Mike replied.

"Uh-huh," Lily answered. "Ashley taught her how."

"Who's Ashley?"

"Me!" said one of Lily's friends, a gamine child with long red hair and a riot of freckles dotting her nose and cheeks.

"You taught Princess a trick?"

Ashley nodded.

"I helped," said a golden-haired pixie.

"Me, too," said the last girl.

"Sounds like you guys have been busy," Mike said. His eyes met Angelina's over the heads of the children, and their gazes locked in a significant exchange. An adult exchange. The silent exchange of lovers.

"Don't you want to shake hands with Princess?" Lily asked.

"I'll, uh, take care of these while you're playing with the puppy," Angelina said, abandoning him to the mercy of the girls.

It took Angelina a bit longer than anticipated to repair the seam because she had to change thread colors and fill a bobbin with black thread before she could begin. When she returned to the living room, she found Mike seated in the overstuffed armchair with Lily and the puppy in his lap and Lily's friends perched on the arms of the chair while they all watched a video.

Angelina's breath caught in her throat as she took in the tableau. He probably didn't even realize that he was in daddy mode again; it was as much a part of his nature as his easy smile and his gentle touch with animals.

Heartbreaker, she thought. It wasn't fair. He didn't even have to work at it. All he had to do was . . . be himself, and she—

What a fool she'd been to believe she could enter into a relationship so intimate and remain emotionally aloof! She'd told herself it would be fun—just a little fling, a brief affair. Companionship and physical fulfillment without strings or lasting repercussions. *Convenient. Temporary. Uncomplicated.*

Thinking back on it, she was awed by her naiveté. She'd dated only casually before she met Thomas, and they'd become lovers only after they were engaged. She hadn't been on a date since her divorce. What had made her believe, even for a moment, that she could do an abrupt turnabout and treat a relationship as though it were nothing more than passing a few hours in a man's company?

Although she'd been fighting the idea—it was just too serious, and too scary—she could no longer deny that she had fallen in love with him. *Love* was the only word with the capacity to define her feelings for him: the catch in her chest when he smiled at her; the warmth that tingled through her when she thought of being with him; the contentment that filled her when he put his arms around her.

The lovemaking was thrilling and sweet, but her attraction to him wasn't just physical. She was drawn to his kindness as surely as she was to his maleness, to his gentleness as surely as his strength.

He caught her watching him and grinned sheepishly. She held up the hanger and gave him a thumbs-up. Then she gestured toward the kitchen with a tilt of her head.

Mike whispered something in Lily's ear that made her giggle, then he rose, easing Lily, with the puppy in her arms, down into the seat of the chair.

In the kitchen, Angelina draped the folded pants over the back of a chair. "These are good as new."

He was looking at her face intently, and his smile, warm and sensual, made Angelina aware of his maleness. It turned into a grin. "Thanks for rescuing me."

Angelina shrugged away his gratitude. "It really wasn't a lot of work. Or trouble."

"I suppose someone in the wedding party could have done something with a needle and thread tomorrow, but you know how weddings are. It would have been adding chaos to mayhem."

"Do you have time for a cup of spiced tea?"

"A glass of milk?" he countered hopefully.

"Easier still," Angelina said, opening the cupboard for glasses. She took the milk from the refrigerator. As she poured, she asked, "Do you like the man your sister's marrying?"

"Yes," Mike replied. "Everyone in the family likes him. He and Tracy are great together. She's . . . intense sometimes, and he helps her keep things in perspective."

"I thought maybe you were afraid she was making a mistake."

He cocked his head inquisitively. "What gave you that impression?"

"You seem, well, it's obvious you're not looking forward to the wedding."

The comment drew a frown. "Weddings aren't my favorite form of weekend entertainment," he said.

"I don't think I have to ask what is," Angelina said with a sly smile. To say they'd spent the previous weekend making love was not strictly accurate. They'd taken time out for meals and catnaps, even a rented movie, which they'd watched while cuddled up on the sofa. But when Angelina thought of the day and a half they'd spent together, it was the lovemaking she remembered, the tender touches and whispered endearments.

"I've missed you all week," he said.

The mere sound of his voice was enough to send warmth radiating through her.

"I've thought of you, too," she confessed softly, taking the lid from a cookie jar shaped like a cow and offering him the contents. "Vanilla wafer?"

Mike took a cookie and leaned against the counter as he ate it.

"Why don't you like weddings?" Angelina asked.

"Besides having to wear a tuxedo?" he quipped, dipping his hand into the cookie jar for another vanilla wafer.

"I'm surprised they didn't have the rehearsal tonight, if the wedding's tomorrow," Angelina said.

"The minister performing the ceremony has two weddings back-to-back tonight, so they're having the rehearsal tomorrow morning—without the groom, of course. The best man will take notes and steer the groom through the ceremony."

His gaze settled on Angelina's face, and it seemed to Angelina that the silence that followed lasted an eternity. "Come with me," he said at last.

"To your sister's wedding?"

"Lily, too."

"Lily and I don't belong there, Mike. We've never even met your sister."

He grasped her upper arms. "You'd be my guests. I promise, you'd be welcome."

Releasing a sigh, she bowed her head until her forehead pressed into his sternum. "All this discussion is irrelevant, anyway, Mike. Even assuming I had a suitable dress hanging in the closet all cleaned and pressed *and* the right color stockings to wear with it, it's impossible. This is Lily's weekend at home. Her friends are spending the night. I'm not going to kick them out at the crack of dawn."

Mike's arms slid around her, pulling her into a loose hug. "I should have thought of it earlier."

Yes, Angelina thought. *You should have.*

"I just suddenly realized how much it would mean to have you with me. This wedding . . . The fact is, I was engaged last year and—"

He took a breath and started over. She felt the tension come into his body as he spoke. "It ended just days before the wedding, so everyone's going to be watching me to make sure I'm up to the whole thing."

"Are you?" Angelina asked softly. The question was a gamble; she wasn't certain she wanted to hear about it if he was still nursing a broken heart over the woman he'd almost married.

"Yes!" he said as though suddenly realizing it himself. Nodding incredulously, he said, "Yes. I'm okay with it. I'm happy for Tracy. I don't even mind my baby sister beating me to the altar."

Looking straight into her eyes, he smiled. "I wish you were going. I'm sorry I didn't think of it in time."

"It wouldn't have been a good idea, anyway," Angelina said. "Weddings are a family thing. What would your family think if you showed up with a total stranger and a child?"

"They'd think—no, they'd *know*—that you were important to me."

"It's way too soon for that kind of—"

Easing her away from him slightly, he cradled her chin and guided her face up until their eyes met. "You're important to me, Angelina. That's a fact. And Lily is important to me because she's part of you. Please don't try to pretend that I'm imagining what's going on between us."

She couldn't pretend in front of him, not when her feelings were so close to the surface. She could not even deny him—despite the four children in the next room—the kiss that suddenly seemed to her as inevitable as the ebb and flow of the ocean.

12

MIKE STOOD with his sister and mother in the church anteroom where brides waited for the cue to go down the aisle.

His mother shook an imaginary crimp from the sheer fabric of Tracy's veil, then sighed as she gave her daughter an affectionate inspection. "I just wish your father were still alive to see how pretty you are," she said.

"He's probably watching," Tracy said. "If I know Daddy, he'd find a way."

Mrs. Calder grinned wryly. "You're probably right."

She turned her attention to Mike. "And I was right about the tuxedos, wasn't I? Look how stunning Mike is."

"I could take numbers from the girls on campus who'd be willing to go out with him," Tracy said.

Mrs. Calder's face turned tragic as she patted Mike's arm. "It's just too bad your own plans didn't work out, or we'd have seen you in a tux sooner. It's not too painful for you, is it, being here with all these wedding trappings?"

"No," he said as Tracy sent him a sympathetic look through her veil. "I'm over the whole thing now, Mother. In fact, it was probably for the best. Beth Ann wasn't the woman for me."

Tracy's jaw dropped as she caught his involuntary grin. But just as she opened her mouth to speak, there was a knock at the door. It was the groomsman assigned to escort the mother of the bride to the proper seat. "It's time, Mrs. Calder," he said. "Whenever you're ready."

Mrs. Calder nodded to the young man, then hugged both her children before placing her gloved hand on the groomsman's folded arm and allowing him to lead her away.

Tracy turned to Mike. "What gives?"

"What do you mean, what gives?"

"That goofy grin when you said Beth Ann wasn't for you. You've found another woman, haven't you?"

Mike's face confirmed it, but he hedged. "Aren't we supposed to be going out to listen for our cue?"

"Yes," Tracy said. "But don't think you're off the hook. I want details during the reception."

"How about a hug for your big brother before I have to give you to what's-his-name?"

"You know his name as well as I do," Tracy said, hugging him. "And I still want details!"

"Women!" Mike said.

"I'm just so happy for you!" she said. "Now I don't have to feel so guilty about being so happy myself."

"You always did talk too much," Mike teased. "Come on. What's-his-name is waiting."

Later, at the reception, he found he didn't mind talking about Angelina at all. Or Lily.

"You should have brought them to the wedding," Mrs. Calder said after hearing him speak so fondly of them.

"You're right, Mother," he replied. "I should have." Then, with a mischievous smile, he added, "Maybe I'll bring them to the next wedding I go to."

LILY WAS ABOUT to wiggle out from under the seat belt, she was so excited. "What kind of surprise?"

"I don't know, sweetie," Angelina said. "Dr. Mike just said that I should bring you to his office on our way home because he had a very special surprise for you."

Lily was thoughtful a moment. "Do you think it's a kitten?"

If Dr. Mike Calder values his life, it won't be a kitten! Angelina thought. "Dr. Mike knows you have a puppy, Lily. He knows you don't need a kitten."

"Ashley has a kitten and she has two dogs."

Good for Ashley! Angelina thought, her chest tightening with the irrational sense of inadequacy mothers sometimes suffer when children make unreasonable demands. She let the comment about the menagerie at Ashley's house slide by.

Upon their arrival at Mike's office, Lily was out of the car the instant Angelina turned off the engine. Angelina could only shake her head in awe as she watched her daughter sprint to the building.

Lily was conferring with Suzie at the reception counter when Angelina entered the office. Suzie greeted Angelina. "I was just telling Lily that Dr. Calder is expecting you, but he's with a patient. He said you could come on back and see what's in his boarding room."

"Is it something alive?" Lily asked as Suzie led them into a room lined on one side with wire crates, on the other by two chain-link pens, a small sink and cabinet area.

"Come see," Suzie said, kneeling beside a cardboard box.

Lily peered into the box and gasped. "Raccoons! Look, Mommy! Little bitty raccoons!"

The babies were curled into little balls, sleeping, on an old towel. "Can we hold them?" Lily asked.

Suzie raised a stern eyebrow. "You'll have to talk to Dr. Mike about that. They can't be handled much. They shouldn't be without their mother yet, but their mommy was hit by a car. A man dropped them off this morning. They lived behind his house. When he saw the mother get hit, he went out looking for the babies and brought them to us hoping we could take care of them."

She looked at Angelina. "I'd better get back to the desk. Mike will be in as soon as he finishes with his last patient."

"Aren't they sweet, Mommy?" Lily said, turning to Angelina with a beatific smile.

"Yes," she said, her throat tight as she looked at her daughter's sweet face. The haunted seriousness that had marred Lily's young features just a few weeks earlier had been replaced by the natural curiosity and innocence of youth.

Mike was partially responsible for the change. It made Angelina's heart swell with gratitude. And it terrified her.

"What do you think of my babies?" Mike asked, entering the room. He was wearing his work uniform—jeans, a T-shirt with the clinic logo and a lab coat.

Lily dashed to him. "They're *so-o-o* little," she said excitedly. "And they're *so-o-o* sweet. Can I hold them?"

"It just so happens," Mike replied, "that they have to be bottle-fed, and I could use some assistance."

He winked at Angelina above Lily's head, and Angelina's breath caught. Such a simple gesture, that wink. Yet it was so intimate.

He sat Lily down in a chair and put the raccoons, nestled in the towel, into her lap. After warming the bottle, he showed her how to hold it at the proper angle.

"Are you going to keep them?" she asked.

"Only until tomorrow," he said. "There's a society that takes care of orphaned animals and then finds homes for them in the forest somewhere."

Lily's eyes didn't leave the little raccoons in her lap as she sighed. "Oh."

"What you're doing right now is very, very important," he told her. "By feeding them this formula, you're helping to keep them healthy until they're big enough to survive on their own."

"I'm going to tell Miss Thornton about this," Lily said.

"I've got my camera in the van. I'll take some pictures so you can take them to school."

By the time he'd finished off the roll of film, the raccoons had finished their formula and gone back to sleep.

"Is it okay if we name them?" Lily asked as Mike transferred the babies, one by one, to the original box.

"I think that would be all right," he said. "What do you want to call them?"

"Wynken, Blynken and Nod," she said. "Because they sleep so much."

"Those are perfect names for them," Mike said. "Wynken, Blynken and Nod." Having settled them into the box, he rose and looked from Lily to Angelina. "Now that they're all fat and happy, why don't I take my two favorite girls out for some pizza?"

"Yeah!" Lily sighed, her face a portrait of delighted surprise.

Mike looked at Angelina. "That's two votes for pizza. What do you say—is it unanimous?"

"I never cook if I can eat pizza instead," Angelina said lightly.

"Just let me get rid of this lab coat," Mike said.

"Lily can wash her hands while you're doing that," Angelina suggested.

"Sure," Mike said, draping his arm across Lily's shoulders. "Come on. You can wash up at my big sink, like a real assistant."

He took her into the utility room, adjusted the water for her and showed her how to pump the liquid soap. As she lathered her hands, he glanced up to see Angelina standing in the doorway, watching him with her daughter. Her eyes were filled with emotion as she smiled approvingly.

Mike returned the smile, thinking how right it felt for her to be in the place he spent the bulk of his time; for her daughter to be here, learning what he could teach her;

for the three of them to be together this way, relaxed and looking forward to a casual outing.

"Are those skeletons?" Lily asked, her interest piqued by a poster featuring several side-by-side photographs of small animals and their skeletal systems.

"Yes," he said, pulling a paper towel from the dispenser and giving it to her. "Dry your hands and I'll show you on the chart how you could tell a cat's bones from a dog's."

He explained the differences, pointing to key areas that differentiated the two. Lily hung on every morsel of information. Her interest in animals delighted him.

He could love this child as easily as he would love one of his own, he thought. Perhaps he already did.

While Mike was busy showing Lily the skeletons, Angelina ventured into the room. The walls were lined with charts and posters, most of which had been produced by pharmaceutical companies. She skimmed the headlines of several before her eyes fell on a sheet of stationery from the manufacturer of a worm capsule. Beneath the logo was a handwritten list of some kind.

Mike Calder's Minimum Requirements for a Woman? Good job...pays well...*no children?* Men scourge upon the earth . . . *new car! sexy!* Angelina Winters, one point five? Samantha, *six!* She could have cried, but she was too furious. She could have screamed, but she was too disappointed.

Mike remembered his drunken manifesto just in time to catch the sudden stiffening of Angelina's spine, a split second before a shudder racked her shoulders and the rhythm of her breathing changed, draining the color from her cheeks.

"I can explain about that," he said, wondering if any explanation would be adequate.

"I don't think I'm up for pizza tonight," she said after an excruciating pause.

"Mommy!"

"Angelina—" Lily and Mike spoke simultaneously.

"I'm not feeling well," Angelina said, jutting out her chin defiantly.

"You should sit down," Mike said, reaching for her. "You look pale."

She jerked her elbow out of his reach. "I just—" She dug into her purse and pulled out her car keys. "I need to go home."

"Lily," Mike said with calm authority, "I think your mommy needs to rest. I'm going to take her into my office and let her sit in the big chair behind my desk."

"Aren't we going to eat pizza?"

"No!" Angelina said.

"There's a kitty in one of the crates in the boarding room where the baby raccoons are. Did you notice her?"

Lily shook her head somberly.

"She's a nice kitty, but she's old and has to have medication every day. We're boarding her for a couple of weeks. She's pretty lonely. Why don't you go talk to her while I take care of your mommy? Her name is Socks."

"Okay," Lily said.

She left the room, and Mike and Angelina stared silently at each other for a moment. "Let's go into my office," he said.

"I don't want to go anywhere with you," she replied coldly.

"You need to sit down."

"I need to go home."

"We have to talk about that stupid list."

"It explains so much," she said, almost as though talking to herself.

"Yes," he said. "But it's not what you're thinking." He grabbed her hand and spoke in a tense whisper. "Maybe you don't want to sit down, but I want some privacy. We have to talk, and I want it between you and me, and not between you, me and your daughter."

She capitulated, and went with him to his office. He shut the door and, once more, they stared mutely at each other.

"When I wrote that list—" He broke off, not knowing where to start.

"I kept thinking you'd call me, but you never did," she said, then gave a bark of hysterical laughter. "Of course you didn't. You didn't want a woman with a child, and—" she sucked in a lungful of air and released it "—and bald tires and a worn-out washing machine."

"The woman I'd been engaged to—"

"Why?" she asked, imbuing the word with misery as her eyes met his accusingly. "Why did you keep doing things for me? I never asked . . . I never *wanted* you to do anything for me."

"I was drunk when I made out that stupid list. It was supposed to have been my wedding day, and I'd been . . . I'd been a bad judge of character, and I was . . . hurting. I didn't want—"

"You didn't want me! Or anyone like me."

"I didn't want anyone like Beth Ann, the woman I'd been engaged to. And you're not like her. Not at all. Once I realized that—"

"You kept . . . showing up. You kept coming back, *doing things* for me."

"I couldn't stay away. I tried, but—"

"That night . . . that first night, we . . . oh, God, I can't believe I let . . . that we—" Her breathing was labored, as if she'd been running.

"Made love," he said, reaching for her. "You can say it aloud. That's what it was, Angelina. It was making love. That's why I couldn't stay away from you, and that's why you chose me."

"I was lonely," she said. "I was . . . *frustrated*."

He couldn't stifle a grin. "Yes. You certainly were."

"You were wearing a suit that night. Where had you been?"

"It doesn't matter where I was. The only thing that matters is where I ended up."

"You were with a woman, weren't you? Was it Samantha?"

"How—" Then he remembered the notations on the list, the ratings he'd put there to remind himself what was important—before he'd realized what really was.

"Did you go from her bed into mine?"

"No. Yes, I was with Samantha. I thought—I wanted—but suddenly it was crystal clear to me who I should be with, so I drove to your house."

He swallowed. "I swear, Angelina, I didn't go to your house expecting . . . I just wanted to see you. I wanted to get to know you."

A solitary tear slid down her cheek, and her chin quivered as she fought for composure. "You glued my bed!" she said. "You brought over a clamp and sandpaper and you *fixed* my bed."

She spun away from him, out of his reach. "I've got to go home. I have to get Lily."

"Don't walk out on us," Mike said.

"When my husband walked out, I swore I'd never become dependent on another man as long as I lived. I was doing just fine until I met you, but I was tired, and it was so . . . easy to let you take care of me."

"And I swore I would never let a woman use me again. And I haven't. That's the difference—don't you see it, Angelina? You weren't using me. The things I did for you—it was because I wanted to help you. And letting someone help you doesn't make you dependent. I didn't do anything for you that you couldn't have done yourself." He took a stab at humor. "Except maybe turning off the water."

She was not amused. She was. . .devastated. He could read it in every feature on her face. Part of him died when he realized that he had put that look on her face. "You'd have taken care of that, too, eventually."

"Wouldn't the dispatchers at 9-1-1 have loved that?" she said.

"We're good together," he said. "You helped me, too. With the wedding announcements, and then the pants."

"I have to go." This time, she backed up the words with action, pushing past him to the door. "Lily?" she called from the hallway.

Lily appeared in the hallway. "Are we going to eat pizza?"

"We'll have a pizza delivered to the house," Angelina said.

"Is Dr. Mike coming home with us?"

Mike felt a surge of hope when Angelina looked at him. "I could drive you home. You're upset."

"I'll be fine once I get to the car," she told him.

Once she gets away from me, Mike thought.

"Can I say goodbye to Wynken, Blynken and Nod?" Lily asked pitifully.

Mike's eyes went to Angelina's face as he held his breath waiting on her reply. If Lily was breaking his heart, he could only imagine how Angelina felt.

"Yes," she said tautly. "But hurry."

Lily returned to the boarding room to tell the raccoons goodbye.

This is what Angelina had feared the most. Her daughter was involved, hurt through no fault of her own. Angelina didn't have to say the words. She had only to look at him with that wounded, helpless expression on her face and he could hear her accusations.

"I couldn't let you walk out of here if I didn't think that we'd get this worked out somehow," he said. "Not now, when you're so upset, but later, when you've had a chance to think about us."

She twisted her head, refusing to look at him.

"That list doesn't mean a thing, Angelina. Where I was before I got to your house a month ago doesn't mean a thing, either. The only thing that matters is that I wound up where I was supposed to be that night."

Her only response was a defiant thrust of her chin.

"For what it's worth," he persevered, "I love you. And as long as you're going to be doing a little thinking, you might think about the fact that I love Lily, as well."

"That's not fair!" she cried, whipping her head around to glare at him.

He grinned. "All's fair in love, Angel. And if you think that was unfair, chew on this—the whole time you were telling me about how badly you wanted a baby, the only thing I could think of was how badly I wanted a baby with you."

Tears made her eyes too bright, but she held them in check. For Lily's sake, Mike imagined.

"That was cruel," she said, choking back a sob.

"It was the God's truth," he countered. "The offer's officially on the table, Angel. A ring on your finger, a baby in your belly and a stepdaddy for your daughter. I'll even throw in a typesetting machine so you can set up an office at home. All you have to do is say yes."

"Lily!" she called, near panic.

"I forgot to mention all the sex you want for as long as I'm drawing breath," he added in a low whisper just as Lily stepped into the hallway from the boarding room.

She didn't look at him again as she herded her daughter out of his office. He could only hope that she wasn't leaving his life for good.

He waited ten minutes, then drove past her house to make sure she'd gotten home all right, heaving a sigh of relief when he saw her car in the driveway and the interior lights on in the house.

There was nothing left for him to do now except wait.

13

Lily! Something had happened to Lily!

It was the first thought that crossed Angelina's mind when she saw Thomas's car in her driveway, and it swelled to unbearable proportions when she spied him trying to attach a note to her front door. In all the weekends that Lily had spent with her father, there had never been an occasion necessitating Thomas's coming to her house.

Panic was gnawing like worms at her insides as she parked her car and dashed to him. "Thomas—what? Lily?"

"We've been trying to reach you." Impatience transformed the statement into an accusation.

"I was at the store," she said defensively. Buying groceries. Oh, God, had something had happened to Lily while she was at the store picking out toilet paper and breakfast cereals? "Lily? Is something—"

"Lily's all right. It's the dog."

Angelina's body went into a meltdown of relief. *Lily was all right. She wasn't hurt, wasn't—*

"We tried to tell you. Denise tried to tell you. It's hard enough keeping tabs on four kids without having to worry about a dog."

Lily had begged to take Princess with her on her weekend visit. Ordinarily, Angelina backed up Thomas and Denise's wishes that the dog not be allowed to accompany her, but Lily had been so upset since the incident at Mike's office earlier in the week that Angelina had pressured Denise into allowing Lily to bring Princess just this once.

"What happened?" she asked.

"The kids were playing in the front yard and the dog dashed away after a ball." His features set in a disapproving scowl that made Angelina wonder how she could ever have loved him. "We can teach *children* never to run after a ball, but not a stupid dog."

"What happened?" she prompted.

"Our neighbor was backing out of his driveway and—" His expression hardened into outrage. "If one of the kids had gone after her, it could easily have been one of them."

"Is she—" She couldn't bring herself to say the word as concern about how Lily would react if Princess was gone swept through her.

"No. But she's hurt. Bad. She was yelping and crying like a damn banshee. She nearly scared Denise to death."

"Where's Lily? How did she—"

"Lily's hysterical. Denise looked in the phone book for a 24-hour vet clinic, but your daughter threw a hysterical fit—"

"*Our* daughter," Angelina corrected, wondering if he'd somehow forgotten that Lily was as much his child as her own.

"She *insisted* that no one except this *Dr. Mike* could possibly treat her dog."

"Mike?"

"Ah, yes. I thought as much."

"What do you mean?"

"That love-struck mooning expression on your face confirms my suspicions. You have something going on with this guy, don't you?"

"I don't see that's any business of yours."

"It is if it affects our daughter."

Oh, so she's yours again! Angelina thought. But she didn't want to fight with him. "Where's Lily now? And Princess?"

"His clinic was closed, but she *insisted* on looking up his home number in the book." His inflection turned ugly. "You must be really thick with this guy, because he agreed to meet us at the clinic."

"He's Princess's veterinarian. He would have met any patient there," she said, realizing as she said it that it was true. He was that kind of vet. That kind of person.

"Denise and the kids are there now. We tried several times to call you. Finally, I decided to come over and leave a note so we wouldn't have to stay on the phone all day."

You're all heart, Angelina thought. "How's Lily?"

"How do you think she is? You know how obsessed she is with that puppy."

"I'd better get over there."

"I think so," came out sounding like, "It's about time."

The drive to Mike's office was both the longest and the shortest trip she'd ever taken. Longest because she was anxious to get to Lily and soothe her; shortest because she dreaded the situation she faced. And she wasn't prepared to see Mike again under any circumstances, but particularly when Lily's puppy was hurt and he would be cast in the role of savior or ringer of the death knell.

She could hardly believe that only four days had passed since she'd stood in his office and he'd proposed to her. Not with candles and soft music and wine, of course. He wasn't a man who planned that far ahead. No, he'd proposed in typical Mike fashion: a ring on her finger, a stepdaddy for her daughter, and a baby in her belly. Not to mention her own typesetting equipment and great sex for the rest of her life.

It wasn't exactly the type of proposal that made the evening news features on Valentine Day. But it was Mike. And it was sincere, because Mike was sincere above all else.

She'd missed him more in the past four days than she'd ever missed anyone in her whole life. Was it any wonder her hand was trembling as she reached for the clinic door?

A maelstrom awaited her inside. Denise, cradling the baby in her arms, charged her. "This isn't my fault."

"No one's blaming you," Angelina said, hoping to appease the woman.

But Denise was beyond appeasement. "I told you I couldn't be responsible for that damn dog, but you wouldn't listen. Oh, no. Lily was so upset. Lily *had* to have her puppy with her."

"We're all upset," Angelina said. "Let's not say anything we'll regret."

That at least made Denise stop and think. "I'm not paying any vet bills," she said at last.

Angelina had exhausted her patience. "No one's asking you to, Denise. Just tell me where Lily is."

"She went off to the back with your boyfriend. She wouldn't let that dog out of her sight."

"I've got to find her."

"We're leaving," Denise said. "The boys are supposed to go to a birthday party. They're already late."

"I can handle it from here," Angelina told her, suddenly confident that she could.

She could handle it all—her child, the emergency, her life. It was a liberating feeling, that self-confidence, that inner serenity, the self-knowledge that she was strong and competent. It filled her with largesse. "Thank you for calling the vet and bringing Princess in. I know how hectic your weekends are."

Denise frowned, then spoke softly, "It wasn't my fault."

"It was an accident," Angelina said.

Denise pointed toward the treatment room area. "They're back there."

"I know the way," Angelina said, moving even as she spoke.

She never looked back.

She found Mike and Lily standing next to a treatment table. Princess was lying on the table, deathly still. Angelina knelt with open arms as Lily ran to her.

"Princess got run over by a car and she has a broken leg."

"I know, sweetie. I'm so sorry your puppy is hurt."

"She's going to be okay," Lily said, drawing out of the embrace. "Dr. Mike is going to put a metal pin in her leg so it'll grow back good as new. And he's going to let me help as long as I don't faint."

"*If* it's all right with your mom," Mike reminded.

He spoke to Lily, but his eyes were on Angelina.

She'd wondered how it would be, what it would be like to face him again. All the way to the clinic, she'd wondered. And now she knew: it was perfectly comfortable and wonderful. It was like being with Mike again.

And although she didn't utter so much as a syllable, she told him yes at that moment. Yes to Lily helping with the surgery. To the wedding band on her finger. To his becoming Lily's stepfather. To babies of their own. To . . . everything.

The hint of a smile on his mouth and the warmth in his eyes told her that he understood.

"Can I help, Mommy? I won't faint," Lily said.

"Yes," Angelina said, still looking at Mike's face. "You can help. I'll help, too, as long as I don't have to watch."

"That should be interesting," Mike observed wryly. "Surgery by braille."

"She's so still," Angelina said, looking at the puppy.

"She's sedated. I'll use a local on the leg."

"He shaved her leg!" Lily said, a chuckle in her voice. "He says now she can wear a bikini."

"Dr. Mike is silly, sometimes," Angelina said.

"Yeah," Lily agreed, as though being silly was the highest accolade which could be attributed to her hero.

"I have to scrub now," Mike said. "Nurse number one—that's you, Lily—I want you to stand right here and make sure Princess doesn't roll off the table. Nurse number two—" He looked at Angelina. "You can help me scrub."

"This isn't scrubbing," Angelina said in the utility room a few seconds later.

Mike pulled her closer. "Hell of a lot more fun, though."

The kiss linked them emotionally as well as physically, sealing unspoken promises between them. They were both breathless when Mike tore his mouth from hers and peered deeply into her eyes.

He smiled devilishly. "So, Angel—when's the wedding?"

"We'll discuss that after you tell me the whole story behind *Mike Calder's Minimum Requirements for a Woman*," she said.

"You mean that old piece of paper that used to be hanging on the wall above my sink?"

"That's the one."

"I threw it out days ago," he said. "It was obsolete. Didn't you notice that it had been updated?"

Apprehensively, Angelina followed his gaze to the wall she'd been avoiding. And there she saw:

*Mike Calder's Minimum Requirements
for a Woman—Revised edition*

1. Her name will be Angelina.
2. She will have a daughter named Lily.
3. She makes great turkey tetrazzini and serves it with vampire bread.
4. Designs beautiful wedding announcements and sews tuxedo trousers on the spur of the moment.
5. Smiles like an angel.
6. Sexy.

"Those are just the bare minimums," he said, hugging her tighter. "It would be nice if she loved me."

"She does," Angelina said, guiding his face to hers for a kiss.

Epilogue

"THANKS," Tracy whispered into Mike's ear as she gave him a hug of congratulations.

"Thanks for what?" he asked.

"For taking the pressure off!" Tracy said. She tilted her head in the direction of their mother, who had her arm draped over Lily's shoulders like a mother hen protecting a chick. "She's been driving me crazy with the grandkid hints ever since I told her I was getting married, but I want to wait a few years. Now you can take part of the heat."

Her demeanor changed dramatically as Mrs. Calder and Lily approached. "I'm so happy for you, Mike."

"Dr. Mike, did you really cut up a dead possum when you were my age?" Lily asked excitedly.

Mike looked from the earnestness in his new stepdaughter's eyes to the sheepish guilt in his mother's.

"I was performing an autopsy," he replied defensively.

"On road kill," Mrs. Calder said wryly. Then she told Lily, "When he brought that possum home, I knew he'd either turn out to be a veterinarian or a serial killer."

"Mother!"

Mrs. Calder answered his scowl with a squaring of her shoulders. "One of the compensations of putting up with absurd situations with your children is being able to tell your grandchildren all about them."

"I'm glad he's a veterinarian instead of a killer," Lily said.

"So am I!" Mrs. Calder agreed with a chuckle. "Guess all those books about animals and trips to the zoo paid off." She brushed a speck of lint from the dark fabric of Mike's coat, then stepped back to admire him. "I was right about the tuxedo. Even at a small informal wedding, the groom should look dashing. And with a bride as stunning as Angelina—"

"She *is* beautiful, isn't she?" Mike said, his eyes following his mother's to the woman at his side. Angelina was dressed in ivory lace, and her hair framed her face in loose curls.

Mrs. Calder took Angelina's hands in hers. "Yes, she is. Welcome to the family, Angelina." She heaved a healthy sigh as she regarded the two of them. "You look so perfect together."

"We *are* perfect together," Mike said, succumbing to the smile that was quickly becoming a fixed feature on his face.

"And don't forget this little angel," Mrs. Calder said, once more drawing Lily under her wing.

Mike looked at Lily. Outfitted in rows and rows of pink ruffles, she did resemble an angel. He grinned at the child. "We could never forget Lily. She's too noisy."

Mrs. Calder continued, addressing Angelina, "Thank you for sharing your daughter with us." Turning to fix

Mike with a motherly scowl, she added, "It's about time I had a grandchild to spoil rotten."

Mischief slid into Mike's ever-present smile. "Maybe when you have more than one, you won't spoil them quite so much."

"Mommy says now that she and Dr. Mike are married, I can have a baby sister or brother soon," Lily said.

Mike chuckled as Mrs. Calder's jaw dropped. "Yes, Mother, we plan on having a baby. Soon. And if you start bawling again, I'm going to exile you to the bedroom with the dogs!"

"It's perfectly acceptable to cry at a wedding," his mother replied defensively.

"Between you and Suzie and Inez, it was a wonder the minister could hear himself think!" Mike teased. Inez had brought a beautifully wrapped wedding gift about the size of an electric can opener.

"I'd almost given up on you ever getting married," Mrs. Calder told Mike in a lecturing tone. "And it was all so . . . *beautiful*."

"Yes," Mike agreed, putting his arm possessively around Angelina's waist. "It was, wasn't it?"

It had really happened, he thought contentedly. *This time, it was real*.

And it was forever. He felt it right down to the marrow of his bones later as he took Angelina's hand in his for a mad sprint through a shower of birdseed tossed on their heads by people who loved them.

Angelina waved goodbye to Lily until the car carried them out of sight of the house, then settled back in the seat and sighed.

"Happy, Mrs. Calder?" he asked, placing his hand over hers.

"Yes," she said. "But—"

But? Panic hit Mike like a ramrod to the guts. *But?*

"I wouldn't want you to get the wrong idea," she said.

"The wrong idea about what?"

"I know you promised to love me, and to be a good daddy to Lily and to give me all the babies I want and a typesetting machine so I can work at home."

"Yes."

"Well, I wouldn't want you to think I married you for any of that."

Relief swept through him. She was teasing. He could hear it in the tone of her voice. "Oh?"

"I wouldn't want you to think that I married you because I loved you, either."

A beat of silence followed.

"So why did you marry me?" he asked finally, playing along.

Her face broke into a devilish smile. "For the sex, of course."

Mike shrugged philosophically and grinned. "I did promise you that, too, didn't I?"

"Yes, Dr. Calder. You certainly did."

"Well," he said, with a shake of his head, "I guess a man's gotta do what a man's gotta do."

"Yes!" Angelina said. "And often."

Mike laughed from sheer joy. "As often as you like, Angel. As often as you like."

Do you have a secret fantasy?

Ashleigh Frost does. Shy and straitlaced, she'd spent her life being controlled first by domineering parents and then by a no-good husband. All she wants to do now is have a little fun—and fantasy. To bring strong-willed men to their knees, weak from their desire for her. Only then she meets Detective Cade Hawkins and the sparks threaten to singe her. Experience the seduction in Tiffany White's NAUGHTY BY NIGHT in August 1995.

Everybody has a secret fantasy. And you'll find them all in Temptation's exciting new yearlong miniseries, Secret Fantasies. Beginning January 1995, one book each month focuses on the hero or heroine's innermost romantic desires....

MOVE OVER, MELROSE PLACE!

FLYAWAY VACATION SWEEPSTAKES!

This month's destination:

Glamorous LAS VEGAS!

Are you the lucky person who will win a free trip to Las Vegas? Think how much fun it would be to visit world-famous casinos... to see star-studded shows...to enjoy round-the-clock action in the city that never sleeps!

The facing page contains two Official Entry Coupons, as does each of the other books you received this shipment. Complete and return all the entry coupons—**the more times you enter, the better your chances of winning!**

Then keep your fingers crossed, because you'll find out by August 15, 1995 if you're the winner! If you are, here's what you'll get:

- Round-trip airfare for two to exciting Las Vegas!
- 4 days/3 nights at a fabulous first-class hotel!
- $500.00 pocket money for meals and entertainment!

Remember: The more times you enter, the better your chances of winning!*

*NO PURCHASE OR OBLIGATION TO CONTINUE BEING A SUBSCRIBER NECESSARY TO ENTER. SEE REVERSE SIDE OF ANY ENTRY COUPON FOR ALTERNATIVE MEANS OF ENTRY.

VLV KAL

FLYAWAY VACATION
SWEEPSTAKES
OFFICIAL ENTRY COUPON

This entry must be received by: JULY 30, 1995
This month's winner will be notified by: AUGUST 15, 1995
Trip must be taken between: SEPTEMBER 30, 1995-SEPTEMBER 30, 1996

YES, I want to win a vacation for two in Las Vegas. I understand the prize includes round-trip airfare, first-class hotel and $500.00 spending money. Please let me know if I'm the winner!

Name_____

Address _____ Apt. _____

City   State/Prov.   Zip/Postal Code

Account #_____

Return entry with invoice in reply envelope.

© 1995 HARLEQUIN ENTERPRISES LTD.   CLV KAL

FLYAWAY VACATION
SWEEPSTAKES
OFFICIAL ENTRY COUPON

This entry must be received by: JULY 30, 1995
This month's winner will be notified by: AUGUST 15, 1995
Trip must be taken between: SEPTEMBER 30, 1995-SEPTEMBER 30, 1996

YES, I want to win a vacation for two in Las Vegas. I understand the prize includes round-trip airfare, first-class hotel and $500.00 spending money. Please let me know if I'm the winner!

Name_____

Address _____ Apt. _____

City   State/Prov.   Zip/Postal Code

Account #_____

Return entry with invoice in reply envelope.

© 1995 HARLEQUIN ENTERPRISES LTD.   CLV KAL

OFFICIAL RULES

FLYAWAY VACATION SWEEPSTAKES 3449

NO PURCHASE OR OBLIGATION NECESSARY

Three Harlequin Reader Service 1995 shipments will contain respectively, coupons for entry into three different prize drawings, one for a trip for two to San Francisco, another for a trip for two to Las Vegas and the third for a trip for two to Orlando, Florida. To enter any drawing using an Entry Coupon, simply complete and mail according to directions.

There is no obligation to continue using the Reader Service to enter and be eligible for any prize drawing. You may also enter any drawing by hand printing the words "Flyaway Vacation," your name and address on a 3"x5" card and the destination of the prize you wish that entry to be considered for (i.e., San Francisco trip, Las Vegas trip or Orlando trip). Send your 3"x5" entries via first-class mail (limit: one entry per envelope) to: Flyaway Vacation Sweepstakes 3449, c/o Prize Destination you wish that entry to be considered for, P.O. Box 1315, Buffalo, NY 14269-1315, USA or P.O. Box 610, Fort Erie, Ontario L2A 5X3, Canada.

To be eligible for the San Francisco trip, entries must be received by 5/30/95; for the Las Vegas trip, 7/30/95; and for the Orlando trip, 9/30/95.

Winners will be determined in random drawings conducted under the supervision of D.L. Blair, Inc., an independent judging organization whose decisions are final, from among all eligible entries received for that drawing. San Francisco trip prize includes round-trip airfare for two, 4-day/3-night weekend accommodations at a first-class hotel, and $500 in cash (trip must be taken between 7/30/95—7/30/96, approximate prize value—$3,500); Las Vegas trip includes round-trip airfare for two, 4-day/3-night weekend accommodations at a first-class hotel, and $500 in cash (trip must be taken between 9/30/95—9/30/96, approximate prize value—$3,500); Orlando trip includes round-trip airfare for two, 4-day/3-night weekend accommodations at a first-class hotel, and $500 in cash (trip must be taken between 11/30/95—11/30/96, approximate prize value—$3,500). All travelers must sign and return a Release of Liability prior to travel. Hotel accommodations and flights are subject to accommodation and schedule availability. Sweepstakes open to residents of the U.S. (except Puerto Rico) and Canada, 18 years of age or older. Employees and immediate family members of Harlequin Enterprises, Ltd., D.L. Blair, Inc., their affiliates, subsidiaries and all other agencies, entities and persons connected with the use, marketing or conduct of this sweepstakes are not eligible. Odds of winning a prize are dependent upon the number of eligible entries received for that drawing. Prize drawing and winner notification for each drawing will occur no later than 15 days after deadline for entry eligibility for that drawing. Limit: one prize to an individual, family or organization. All applicable laws and regulations apply. Sweepstakes offer void wherever prohibited by law. Any litigation within the province of Quebec respecting the conduct and awarding of the prizes in this sweepstakes must be submitted to the Regies des loteries et Courses du Quebec. In order to win a prize, residents of Canada will be required to correctly answer a time-limited arithmetical skill-testing question. Value of prizes are in U.S. currency.

Winners will be obligated to sign and return an Affidavit of Eligibility within 30 days of notification. In the event of noncompliance within this time period, prize may not be awarded. If any prize or prize notification is returned as undeliverable, that prize will not be awarded. By acceptance of a prize, winner consents to use of his/her name, photograph or other likeness for purposes of advertising, trade and promotion on behalf of Harlequin Enterprises, Ltd., without further compensation, unless prohibited by law.

For the names of prizewinners (available after 12/31/95), send a self-addressed, stamped envelope to: Flyaway Vacation Sweepstakes 3449 Winners, P.O. Box 4200, Blair, NE 68009.

RVC KAL